MISS GEORGINA'S CURE

When Georgina's path crosses with that of William Philip Carter's horse, her life takes a dramatic and unexpected turn for the better. The affluent and mysterious Mr Carter placates her anxious mother and takes both of them into his manor house. Unwittingly, he is forced to face dark shadows from his own past. He has rescued Georgina from life with her impoverished family, the result of selfish and weak menfolk: an act which will change his own world forever . . .

VALERIE HOLMES

MISS GEORGINA'S CURE

Complete and Unabridged

LINFORD
Leicester

First published in Great Britain in 2007

First Linford Edition
published 2008

British Library CIP Data

Holmes, Valerie
   Miss Georgina's cure.—Large print ed.—
Linford romance library
1. Love stories
2. Large type books
I. Title
823.9'2 [F]

ISBN 978–1–84782–181–2

Published by
F. A. Thorpe (Publishing)
Anstey, Leicestershire

Set by Words & Graphics Ltd.
Anstey, Leicestershire
Printed and bound in Great Britain by
T. J. International Ltd., Padstow, Cornwall

This book is printed on acid-free paper

1

'You just don't trust me, girl! That's your problem, and me your own ma!' Agatha bundled up her bits of clean rags, ointments and vinegar and put them back into the chest that she always kept under her bed, ready for the next emergency. She was smiling to herself and Georgina knew it, because with her there always was another time.

'It's not that I don't trust you, it's just that the cure, as you call it, hurts more than the original injury — usually.' Georgina put her head into her hands as her mother cleaned up the scrape on her knee. 'It's because it stings so.'

When the bandage was tied in place, Georgina placed her foot carefully back down on the cold flagged stone floor. Her skirts were rolled up above her knees, one of which was now bandaged. She had felt so secure in the tree that she could not understand how she had come to fall out of it.

'Georgina, how many times do I need to tell you that you are just too big now for such antics? You were too big for that sort of thing at twelve, but now at nearly twenty — you are becoming 'odd'. It's just not done for a young woman to be so active. What if you'd been seen by Mrs Crabtree?

'The gossip would be all around the kitchens of the big house and you'd never stand a chance of gettin' a position up there. Look, I heard as how they will be takin' on more staff soon now that spring is nearly here.'

Georgina watched her mother, her mood had changed again. She was angry with her for she could have injured herself and stopped the chance of working up at the 'big house' — because she had fallen from the tree.

'That would be such a shame,

wouldn't it?' Georgina answered provocatively, not caring a bit as she did not want to work up at the 'big house' caged in like an animal and working just as hard as one. It was not for her. She had it firmly in her mind what she could do.

'Lass, I should knock that smirk from your selfish little face.' Her mother placed a hand firmly on each of her ample hips and stared at her. 'We could do with the extra money. You've not got yersel' a young man yet. Jeb Duncan is always lookin' at yer, and . . . '

'Jeb! That big oaf. He doesn't know the difference between a good woman and a prize cod. They're both just a catch to him, that's where his thinking stops.' Georgie smiled but her ma flushed a deeper pink.

'He's a strong, fit young man who'd think he'd potted the best fish in the sea if you so much as paid him any attention.'

'That's exactly what I mean, Ma. I want someone who will love me for what I am, not what they think I should be.' Georgina folded her arms across her body.

'You learn to love. Only the few can be so picky, lass.' Her ma looked at her with a much calmer understanding manner. Georgina thought that her time to broach the sensitive subject again was now.

'I'd be better off with Pa, fishing. I'd make a much better fisherman than ever our Daniel will. He can't look at a boat without turning green in the face.' Georgie laughed but her mother did not. Georgie realised that this was not the right time. 'Ma, you know how much I like being out in the boat.'

'That does it! It is time that your arrogant little head had its eyes opened wide. Wash up and wrap yourself up in yer shawl, yer comin' with me!' Her ma reached for her own old woollen shawl and waited for Georgina by the small cottage doors. Her arms were folded and her manner absolute. Georgie realised she was now in trouble.

'Ma, I can't walk, my knees are right sore. Yer can't make me walk now, can you?' Her words were having no effect upon her mother's resolve. She limped towards her, heavily, badly even, over stressing her injury and frowning.

Her mother opened the door. Georgina had lost the point of her argument so reluctantly she walked out into the bracing sea breeze. It refreshed her instantly and she felt full of life once more, but her mother pulled her arm and she was turned away from the flat and sandy beach and led up the road through town and out at the other side.

The town was slowly developing into a notable size. What had once been a row of low-lying fishing cottages now had its own coach house, store, clothiers, dispenser, church and boat-house. New houses were dwarfing the old fisherman's dwellings, but not everyone was happy about it.

However, the two inns had plenty of trade. One catered for locals, that was The Angel down by the sand and the other, The Swan, built for the passing trade, along with the *incomers* as the new residents were referred to locally.

The Swan had been renamed The Goose by the locals. Much of the development was down to the influence of the 'big-house' or, to be more specific, the master of the newly renovated hall, Mr William Philip Carter.

He was rarely seen in the town himself, but when he did ride in on his fine steed he caught the eye of every young maid there. Not Georgina's, though. She could not bear the man's obsession with style and panache. He looked as though he saw straight through the people, unless they were the more affluent 'new' villagers who were moving into the houses.

'Where are we goin' to, Ma?' Georgina was worrying that she was going to be handed into the service of the Carters before she'd even had time to recover from her last bit of fun. Her knee was sore, it did sting and it was bruised. There was no way she could kneel down and scrub floors like that — surely?

'You're here so that those blinkered eyes of yours will see clearly, lass, once and for all.' Her mother stormed off with renewed speed. They left the town and followed the path up to the church on the headland. It was a windswept place.

The place was chosen because the old fishermen wanted to be buried where their bodies could hear the waves of the sea below. Georgina thought that this was rather short-sighted of them as they'd already be dead, so she really couldn't see the point of it. It created more work for everyone, the grave-diggers, the coffin bearers, the families and especially the Reverend Silas Cane.

The man had been putting on weight since he came to Scarbeck. Too many meals with the Carters she suspected. Still, on they climbed until, out of breath, they finally reached the church, but her ma did not stop there. She took her straight to the graveyard.

'Ma, it's blowin' a gale here. If we don't go back they'll find our bodies down in Whitby!' Georgina was exaggerating the strength of the wind. Whitby was a good thirty miles further south down the rugged stretch of coast with its treacherous rocks and sweeping bays.

'Look around you, lass. What do yer see?' Her mother stood there pointing around the graveyard.

'Headstones, crosses . . . graves!' Georgina shouted across, her words almost blown away on the wind.

'People, lass . . . fishermen. Most of these folk died at sea or because of it. Some of these graves are empty, their bodies never given back by the waves. You think I want that for you?'

Her mother walked over to her and put a hand on her arm. 'Georgie, yer me favourite bairn! God forgive me for sayin' so as I shouldn't choose one over another and I'll never repeat it again, but don't ever get in a boat on that treacherous mass of water. I may lose yer pa to it one day, or even that good-for-nothin' brother of yours, but not you. You are born for better.'

Georgina was speechless. She had never heard her ma talk to her in such a way before. It was so . . . honest. Georgie hugged the woman and kissed her cheek.

'Oh now, don't go gettin' all soft like. Whatever will people say? You go and get a job up at the house. You know yer letters and yer manners. I'll wager you'll be as fine as the Carters themselves one day. Yer special, yer different and always have been. Now, go on ahead and make me a good hot drink as, by the time I climb back down there, I'll be needin' it; and not a word to a soul about this, yer hear.'

'About what, Ma?' Georgie asked and shrugged her shoulders as her ma laughed at her. She could always make her mother happy and that, Georgie guessed, was why she was special to her, as her father and brothers never paid her much attention at all, only talking about their fishing trips, the catch made and the 'incomers'.

Georgina ran down most of the steep slope of the cliff path and straight out into the road.

She had meant to stop, but with the wind on her back and the speed she was running she couldn't. Her dark chocolate brown hair that had been tied neatly at the nape of her neck was half loose and hung over one shoulder. She carried her bonnet in her hand as the wind had long since blown it from her head.

It was almost without any feeling at all that she found herself on the sandy track face down. Her world swirled around her and she couldn't seem to lift herself up. Voices were echoing around her, a deep man's voice and the distant shouts of a woman. She thought she knew the woman's voice, but everything seemed confused until she slipped off into sleep.

'What have yer done to me bairn,

man?' Agatha screamed up at the rider of the fine horse. She was near to being hysterical.

William Phillip Carter had already dismounted. He could not believe what had just happened. It was with great relief that he saw the girl was still breathing.

He spoke to the young woman who had nearly unseated him as she ran out into the road from the direction of the cliff path.

The horse had reared and the girl screamed, falling down and hitting her head on the hard ground.

'She ran out into the road at speed. I could not have missed her, ma'am. It was she who ran into me!' He was bending over her, turning Georgina's limp body over carefully on his arm. A mark on her forehead told him what he needed to know. She had hit her head and was concussed.

He looked at her and realised that she was much older than at first he had imagined. Like the older woman had called her 'her bairn', he also had thought her to be a child, but she was in fact a pretty young woman.

'Is she . . . ? Oh, man, let me have a look at her.' Agatha bent down next to her and started to try to shake her awake. The man looked at her sternly.

'Cease!' William was incensed that the wench was so ignorant that she did not realise the harm she could do the girl.

'That's me daughter and you have no right injurin' her and then interferin' when I wants to help her,' Agatha protested. She looked desperate and near to panic.

William stood to his full height with Georgina held in his arms. She was light and he suspected underfed.

The locals he viewed as ignorant, and from what this woman had just done he was convinced that his opinion of them was valid.

'So, you are the girl's mother?' he asked, as he looked down on Agatha's worried face.

The woman was obviously over-whelmed with her emotions and concerned, so he would, he decided, forgive her ludicrous outburst.

'Yes, and she must be all right — she has to be!' Agatha, he could see was close to tears.

'I shall go to the coach-house and we shall have her taken safely up to Carlton Hall where she will be fully examined, rested and treated, if necessary, for her injuries.'

'I'm her mother . . . ' Agatha began to protest.

'Yes, we have established that fact.' He turned and looked at her sternly.

'I demand that I accompany her and see she is treated right,' Agatha almost shouted the words up at him.

His eyes fixed upon her. 'You have a choice, ma'am. You either give your blessing that she is taken to a place of safety and seen to by a qualified physician who has trained in the University of Edinburgh, or you take her home and let the local saw-bones loose with her and live with the consequences and costs.

'If she comes with me now, however, there will be no cost incurred to yourself, and her food and keep will be the best anyone could expect until she is fully restored to her former irresponsible self.

'Now be quick and make up your mind as this is wasting my time and more importantly slowing down her recovery.'

He watched as the woman looked at the girl in his arms, and stroked her hair fondly. She was worried and wanted to stay with her, but it was more important to William that he be allowed to examine her unhindered by an interfering matriarchal figure, so unfairly, he knew, he was using his position to separate the two. William suspected she may have injured her leg when she clashed with Titan, his mount.

'You'll see she's treated right . . . sir?' The woman's eyes were watering.

William softened his attitude towards her a little. 'Ma'am, if you arrive at the coach-house at ten o'clock in the morning I shall send a carriage for you and you can visit her, to allay your fears for her safety and to ascertain the prognosis.'

She looked at him blankly as he spoke.

'To find out what is wrong with her. Then, we shall talk again. For now, look after your other family members and I will talk to you tomorrow.' He waited for her to look at him, but her eyes were fixed upon the girl. Eventually she looked up at him and nodded. They had approached the gates of the coach-house.

'Stephens!' he shouted, 'there has been an accident. Can you go and retrieve Titan from the north road and ride him to the Hall for me . . . with great care.' The young man called Stephens face lit up at the thought of riding such a fine animal over the open country to the big estate.

'Yes, sir,' he shouted out and was gone as quick as a flash.

Another man helped him to lay

15

Georgina down in the back of a canvas covered, drab painted moors wagon. He climbed up into the driver's seat and took the reins in his hands.

Agatha was standing with sad puppy-dog eyes by the coach-house doors. He moved the wagon forward until he was level with her mother.

'Woman, climb in the back with your daughter. You can keep her steady until we arrive at the Hall and Stephens will bring you back here with the cart, but that is my final word on the matter, do you hear?' He smiled at her, try to smooth away the woman's pain.

He could see the fear in her eyes as she saw the wagon with her child in it, for he knew that she was desperately worried about her.

'Yes, sir.' Agatha stumbled and struggled until she managed to climb on board and huddle next to Georgina.

'Shake her ma'am and I'll toss you off the wagon. You keep her steady, that's all. It is the best thing you can do for her.'

Agatha nodded frantically. 'I just couldn't bear to lose her. She's so loving and intelligent. She's more like one of your type than ours. She don't rightly fit in the village, but she's good, sir, and special.'

The woman sniffed and William found himself watching her in amazement. 'Eee, our lass, when I said I wanted you to work up at the big house, I never dreamed you'd end up there so soon and like this!' Her words were whispered, but William understood them all the same. It was the first time he had heard his home referred to in that manner.

'What is her name?' he asked.

'Georgina, sir,' Agatha answered.

'That's unusual for a local girl, isn't it?' he asked, not that he knew many of the locals, but he imagined they would be a Sally, Nellie or Beth.

'It's special,' Agatha replied and he could sense the pride in the woman's voice, 'like my Georgie, she's a special person. She has energy and deserves a better life. Never known a girl who could handle a coble with her brothers. People don't like women to be able to do stuff like that, but my Georgina is gifted, sir, she deserves better.'

The woman was cradling her daughter's head, and William listened, amazed at the words of the woman. Was she talking through grief? Or pitching a case for him to help the young lass find a way out of the drudgery of a fisherwoman's life? He had no idea, but his greatest concern was that she had a life to live, whether as maid or wife to a fisherman raising a brood of children on a meagre existence. First, she had to recover.

He glanced down at the beautiful young woman laid out in the back of the wagon and he could see she was everything her mother thought she was in looks. He had already discovered she had a spirit, and a lively carefree nature, he just hoped that she would soon be the same again.

With knocks to the head, he had

discovered from the experience of his work amongst the miners of the northern coalfields that there were no guarantees. Only time and the good Lord would show him what her fate would be.

2

Carter drove the wagon through the gateway to the 'big-house'. He was proud of what he had achieved here. The once crumbling walls, that surrounded the vast grounds from the strong north-easterlies, and rusty gates were now rebuilt or replaced.

As he steered the wagon between the new iron gates he picked up speed on the now smooth driveway. He had the new road-making materials that were revolutionising other parts of the country's road system brought to the Hall as a showpiece of what was possible, but they had not been used in this far flung corner of the country — which was why he had chosen it. He drove around the large fountain in front of the Hall, ironically enough it had a horse rearing up on its hind legs in the centre of it.

The woman still held her daughter's hand and all along the journey she had whispered to her, affirming her love and telling the girl how she deserved so much more in life than she could give her. The mother's eyes were fixed upon her daughter's face. William felt for her, he knew compassion was his weakness, but he was going to be firm with her for the young woman's sake.

They pulled up outside the Hall. Stephens was sitting on the steps awaiting the arrival of the wagon. He stood as soon as he saw Mister Carter approach.

'Did you return Titan safely to his stall without incident?' Carter asked, as he jumped down from the driver's seat.

'Yes, sir.' The man smiled at him, obviously having enjoyed the experience. William knew he was a confident rider and that was why he allowed him to ride his pride and joy.

'Good,' he said firmly, not showing his inner relief.

A servant ran down the steps from

the Hall's large doors. 'Mister Carlton, what happened to you, sir?'

'Benson, I have an injured girl here. Fetch Higgins to help you carry her in and tell Martha to prepare the governess's bed in the nursery.'

Agatha glanced up at him with a questioning look as the man ran off to carry out his instructions.

'I do not have a governess at present. It will be the warmest and most cheerful room for her to recover in. Does that meet with your approval?'

He raised an eyebrow.

'Yes, sir. I thought you'd put her in the servants' rooms. I never dreamt you'd see her well in your own house . . . Hall. Thank you,' she added.

'The governess's bed is a servant's bed, it just happens to be in the main Hall rooms.' He nodded to acknowledge her thanks, but was determined not to appear a soft touch by these people. He wanted to be known as fair but firm.

The men came and he instructed that

they carry her up the stairs with great care. He saw the mother watch her disappear beyond the doors.

'Now, ma'am. You return with Stephens and in the morning at ten o'clock I will send my carriage to the coach-house for you and you can see how your daughter is then — as we agreed.'

She stared at him. Her eyes moist with her unshed tears, but he had resolved not to give in to sentimental feelings. She nodded agreement.

'She will be fine? I mean she has just been knocked out, hasn't she?' There was a plea in her voice.

'I hope so. However, I need to attend her and you should return to your family.' He was about to turn away from her as Stephens took up the reins of the horse and climbed up onto the wagon.

'Sir, you said she'd be seen by the physician.' The woman was looking at him suspiciously; there was a lack of trust between them, and the classes they belonged to.

'And indeed she will. Good day, ma'am.'

He climbed up the stairs two at a time. Carter had no wish to explain to her that it was he who was the physician. He had left that life far behind him and all the pain that remembering what had happened was brought back to him. It was not one he had ever wanted to return to.

He was annoyed that he had no choice, other than to turn the girl over to the saw-bones in the village, as he had seen what Archibald Pratt was capable — or not capable of. It was time that such butchers were stopped from preying on the ignorant and vulnerable like this woman and her mother.

As he entered the hall he discarded his hat and coat and ran up the stairs to the nursery rooms on the second landing. The two men had laid her carefully on the bed and were descending as he reached the top.

'Send Millie, with warm water and

two clean nightgowns.' He entered the room and the girl was still lying there, breathing evenly, but not yet conscious. This was worrying him.

He stood at the bottom of the bed and looked at her. First he pulled the off the badly worn out boots. They had been mended and resoled, until they were threatening to fall apart on the foot. He discarded them, revealing two feet that were sore from where the boots rubbed her young skin.

When Millie arrived, he smiled at her. Of all the servants in the house, Millie was the only one who had come with him from his previous home and work. She was good, trustworthy and knew how to keep her mouth discreetly shut.

'What happened, sir?' she asked as she placed the bowl of warm water down on the bedside stand and lifted the nightgowns from her arm, placing one on the bed and putting one in a drawer.

'This girl ran out in front of Titan. I

avoided trampling her under hoof, but she fell and knocked her head. I know he caught her leg. Millie, we need to get her out of these rags, clean her up and possibly splint this leg. Lock the door, I don't want us to be disturbed.' He glanced at her and she nodded. She knew what he meant and why he had good reason to take such care.

Millie did as she was bid. William and Millie together, removed her dress and then he examined Georgina more carefully. He did not hold with the superficial ideals of propriety. A human body was either one of two sexes. Most of the bodily functions were the same.

Therefore, he helped Millie to change her and in the process was able to ascertain the extent of her bruising and her medical needs. His suspicions were founded, the leg was bruised and there was the possibility that it could be slightly fractured.

'Millie, you clean her and I'll fetch my bag and we'll set the leg. It will pain her, though, so I hope she does not come around before.'

Within minutes of Millie washing her body with a soft cloth and warm soapy water, Georgina's eyes opened.

'Agh!' she let out a scream. She was confused. An image of a big black beast bearing down on her flashed through her mind. Then she realised she was lying on a bed in the middle of a vast, airy, light room. He head ached, with a thumping feeling above her left temple. 'Where am I?' she said as a maid came into her line of vision.

'You are in the Hall, miss. Nothing to worry about here, you'll mend fine. Now let me pull your nightdress nice like.' Millie leaned over her and tugged the nightdress down.

Georgina tried to move away from her, but a sharp pain shot down her right leg.

'Ow! Get off me. What has happened to me?' Georgie was hit by both a feeling of panic and annoyance at the woman as she tugged and fussed at the nightgown until she was respectable again. 'I want my clothes, and I want to go home to me ma. She'll know what to do with me!' Georgina said defiantly, and pushed herself up into a sitting position using all the strength in her arms. To her amazement it was a man's voice who answered her.

'I doubt that, as she could have seriously injured you by trying to shake the life out of you when you fell.' He walked boldly into the room and stood at the foot of the bed with a leather bag under one arm, some clean bandages and a couple of covered wooden things under his other.

He was tall, dark of hair and complexion and, with his sleeves rolled loosely up his arms and his waistcoat hanging open, very handsome.

'How dare you insult me ma, like that.' She couldn't hold herself up anymore. Her arms felt weak, her head was dizzy and her leg hurt so much. Her arms folded and she had to fall back onto the bed. She was very aware that this man was looking at her in a nightgown. Although it was quality fabric and quite thick, she felt extremely ill at ease. She was extremely vulnerable and at the mercy of the two complete strangers.

'I did not insult her, merely stated the truth. She has no medical knowledge worth the knowing.' He put the things down on the end of the bed. Georgina was in a great deal of pain, but did not want to show it.

'And you do know, I suppose,' she said sarcastically.

'Actually, miss, I do. However, you need not worry about that as I shall see you are well whether you deserve such care or not. I suggest you amend your manners and mind your tongue. You are here as my guest, until the effects of your foolish actions are mended.'

'My foolish actions! It was you who ran me down!' Georgina knew she was wrong and should thank him meekly, but she was frightened and, like a trapped animal, she fought back. He was strong in character — like her, she could sense it, and he had power, strength and money on his side and she was helpless.

He flicked the hem of her nightgown up above her knee and she gasped and raised a hand which he caught in one strong fist.

'Woman, you strike me and I'll make you crawl back to your hovel. You are in my home and here we behave differently.' He stared at her with deep brown eyes and she glared back at him.

'Does that include lifting a lady's skirts?' she snapped at him and Millie's face turned cerise.

William laughed. 'You remind me of my horse,' he said casually, as he lay and arranged the splints on the bed and unrolled a length of bandage.

'What?' she asked, not understanding the meaning of his comment.

'You are highly spirited. Now I could break that spirit as you have broken your leg or you could calm down and let me help you. I take it you do want to walk properly again and not become a cripple?' He raised an enquiring brow and then smiled kindly at her as she stared at him speechless for a moment.

She was shocked by his words. She looked at her own leg and tried to move it. It hurt so much that she had to close her eyes with the pain, but she did not cry nor did she scream. The scratches on the other knee seemed nothing to her now.

'Can you fix it?' her voice was softer and her eyes were filled with fear. The thought of not being able to climb trees again because of her age had seemed terrible enough to behold but, now faced with the prospect of not walking properly again, she realised how childish she had been.

'I think so, that is if you do as I say and don't fight me like a wildcat or defy my instructions.' He patted her shoulder and she felt his warmth through the fabric. It was odd to be touched in such a personal way as he did. The town surgeon was old, fat and usually drunk. This man was like gentry. She nodded.

'Good, now this is going to hurt a little, but not for long. Try to relax your body as much as you can. Once we have set the leg, Millie will fetch something to help that head of yours.'

'Like what?' she asked limply, as she watched him position his hand under her ankle, whilst the other felt carefully around her shin bone. Fear of pain had replaced embarrassment and the indignity of what he was doing.

'Something to cool that hot head down,' he smiled at her warmly, distracting her as she laughed at his words then, with one swift pull and what felt like a twist, she screamed.

He continued, with Millie's help, to strap up her leg as quickly and efficiently as they could, whilst Georgie gasped for breath and recovered her composure. Once done, he sent Millie to fetch some ice. This was a very generous gesture, Georgie thought, but she was grateful for it. He held her hand, like her mother would have done.

'You rest it and it will be well. If you

put your weight on it too soon, Georgina, you shall not give it the chance to mend. Be in no hurry to return to your home. I was as much responsible for the accident as you so I will do my bit to restore you to your former glory, if you do yours.'

Their eyes met for a moment and neither said a word as if they were absorbing something of each other. Rather abruptly he stood up and rolled down his sleeves. Then he adjusted the hem of her nightgown down to her ankles, as low as it would go. 'Millie will see to your needs now. So rest and relax, you are safe here.' He picked up his bag and walked towards the door.

'Doctor?' she shouted after him.

He looked surprised as he glanced back at her.

'I am not the doctor. I am William Phillip Carter, your host.' He bowed as if formerly introducing himself.

Georgina was even more surprised by this man that she had heard so many tales about, but what she saw in front of her hardly looked like the ogre she had envisaged.

'Thank you,' she said politely.

He raised a dismissive hand and left her alone in a world that was every child's dream. It was decorated with toys and she loved it, but oh how her leg hurt and she missed her lovely, 'ignorant', ma.

3

Agatha arrived in the carriage that had been sent for her. She was speechless and more than a few heads turned as she, a humble fisherman's wife, stepped up into the grand black carriage. Inside, the leather seats shone as though they had just been polished to perfection. The smell of wax and lavender hung in the air; it was so sweet and different from the smell of old nets or flithers. The footman placed a piece of sack-cloth on the carriage floor before she climbed in. Agatha glared at him feeling insulted, but also aware that the coach was grander than she herself would ever be.

'Sand,' he said, as if offering her a reasonable explanation for his action. The door was closed behind her before she had the chance to sit herself down. The vehicle moved along and she waved to her Bill as she was driven away. Her husband was leaning against a stack of crab pots with his friends and their son, Daniel, all smoking clay pipes and smiling broadly at her.

It all seemed like a dream and that when the coach jolted she would wake up and Georgie would be singing in the cottage as she always did when they made breakfast together, meagre as it was. But when the vehicle jolted she was still in it, so this was no dream.

She would have been really happy if it hadn't been for the sickening fear of losing her precious Georgie, and being left with just her men folk — not that she didn't love them, quite the opposite; they worked hard and drank hard, but Georgie made her laugh, gave her life some meaning amongst the endless toil.

As soon as the carriage stopped by the side of the Hall she climbed out backwards not waiting for the pompous man in the stupid uniform to come around for her. She was halfway up the steps to the Hall's main entrance, before he stepped in front of her blocking her path.

'This way, ma'am.' He pointed down the steps as if she was to accompany him around the back of the large, newly refurbished building. But before she moved, the Hall door was opened by a house servant and the master was standing there beckoning her to come to him.

She looked up at his tall figure. He was wearing a riding outfit that accentuated his handsome frame. He was fit, that was plain to see, no fat or rich man's gut on him. Agatha could not stop herself from thinking that if only her Georgie was a proper lady, and not a fisherman's girl, what a match they would make; him strong in body and her in strength of mind.

Then she pictured her fallen figure, lying stock-still upon the ground, and shook her head. 'God, let her be well', she muttered the prayer to herself for the umpteenth time. It had almost become a chant she repeated it so often.

Her thoughts were interrupted as he bid her good morning.

'Mornin', sir. How's me bairn doin'? She's woke up, has she?' William saw the woman's anxiety on her face.

'Calm yourself, ma'am. Please come inside and we shall talk.' He turned around and led her into the morning room. Tall, rectangular windows gave excellent light to this newly-decorated room. It reflected the master's taste which favoured Josiah Wedgewood's designs.

'Yes, she has woken and is having a hearty breakfast of coddled eggs, ham and freshly-made bread, I believe.' He watched the woman's eyes widen, knowing it would be, to her, food that would feed her whole family.

He could see she was tired, not just through worry about her child, but also by her life. Her hands were coarse and the skin was peeling. She needed some ointment. He fought his natural urge to offer to help her. He must not bring his past here. It was nearly his downfall and he had promised himself that it would never happen again.

'Can she come home now?' she asked nervously.

'No, not yet,' he replied and was not sure if it was relief mixed with the disappointment that he saw on her face. She was busy staring around her, discreetly, at the home he took for granted. He saw her fumble her own grubby skirts, a look of shame crossing her face.

Her dress was coarse, tattered and stretched at the seams.

'She has broken her leg, or rather I should say fractured it. It will need time to heal and, if she is to resume her usual active lifestyle, then it will need to be given time to mend properly and rebuild her strength. The bruise to her head does not appear to have dulled her senses nor curbed her tongue any, though.' He saw a flicker of amusement in the woman's eyes at his last comment, and she bit her lips to quell her own quick witted response.

'I'll see to it she rests it as much as she can,' Agatha replied, obviously doubtful that she would be able to.

'No, you will not. She will stay here until she is free standing, able to walk unaided and run unharmed, and then she may return to her normal duties.' He was sitting opposite her, his fingertips balanced against each other. He watched her closely over the bridge they formed.

'I can't pay for her keep, neither can I fund treatment and I've never taken charity before . . . ' her mother answered defiantly.

'I don't want your money, woman. What need would I have of it?' He flushed slightly and dropped his hands to his lap. 'You are not accepting charity. I am giving her what she needs. It is my own decision and you, ma'am, shall swallow that idiotic pride, because it has no doubt contributed to you being where and what you are today.'

Agatha gasped. 'You may have money and position . . . sir, but you've no right lookin' down on honest workin' folk like that. There's plenty a rich man taken the coin from a poor man and food from his family's starvin' mouths!' She plonked both her hands on her hips and stared at him.

'Really! Well that is one thing I never have and never will do. However, you listen to me now. *Honest* is not what those fishermen are,' he put up a hand, 'Don't defend them or deny it, the trade in contraband grips the whole coast, so do not preach to me. However, your girl will not walk straight again if I let her home with you. I do not want that thought on my mind so I shall see to it she is tended to. Be grateful, woman, and not arrogant.'

He spoke calmly but his meaning settled upon the woman and she sank back into herself, suitably chastised.

'Can I see her, please?' she asked timidly.

'Yes, Millie will take you to freshen

up first and then you may go up to the nursery with her and be returned to your town in two hours time.' He stood up.

'Freshened up?' she queried.

'Yes, I will not have those . . . ' he pointed to her old boots that were covered in wet sand from where she had cut across the beach to save time on her journey to the coach-house at the other side of the bay. The hem of her dress was also damp and ragged. ' . . . sandy boots walking through my home. Millie will see you right, then you may see your daughter so may I suggest you waste no more time. The carriage will leave at one o'clock sharp.' He left the room and Millie entered smiling brightly at her.

Twenty minutes later Agatha came into the bedroom where Georgina lay on the bed staring in wonderment about her. When the door opened she could hardly believe her eyes. 'Ma, is that really you?' Georgie laughed, as they had put her in a dress of the cook's, Mrs Crabtree.

The gown, although a simple brown colour with beige edge trimmings, fitted her properly and a pair of clean boots was on her feet. They had been worn, but as yet not repaired and so to Agatha and Georgina they counted as new. What's more they also fitted her. Her hair had been brushed out and tied up properly and she had had the quickest most thorough wash down of her life.

'Who else do yer think it'd be. Ee, our lass, you scared me 'alf to death. What on earth were yer thinkin' about runnin' away like that.'

Her mother sat down on the large bed next to her then lay back and chuckled. 'Do yer think I should fall down them stairs an' then he might let me sleep here too?' Her mother looked at her then burst into tears, through a mixture of confused emotions — of subdued worry and utter joy.

'What do you think you were doin', runnin' out in the road like that?'

'Oh, Ma, you made me so happy and

I just wanted to run with the wind.'
Georgie leant her head against her
mother's.

'Well, yer won't be runnin' anywhere
for a time. Mr Carter said you're to stay
here until you are fixed.' She looked at
her closely a moment and fingered the
lace on the nightgown. 'He has been
proper with you, hasn't he?'

'Ma! I've broken my leg. What do you
expect him to be doing?' Georgie shook
her head.

'Well, folk is strange and you hear so
many things.' Her mother sniffed as
she always did when she talked about
anything of a too personal nature.

'Well you should stop listening to
them then. No, all he has done is look
after me with the care of Millie. She's
really nice.' Georgie stared out of the
window.

She had not lied. It was true he had
looked after her, she understood why he
and the young maid had been indeli-
cate, but then they had sorted her out.
How could she complain? Feeling the

soft bed, the clean linen beneath her, feeling ill and thinking of her own straw-covered cot at home, Georgie knew where she wanted to stay, at least for now.

The door opened and Agatha jumped up so quickly she nearly fell off the bed. It was Millie with a tray of deliciously-smelling food.

'Mr Carter sends his respects and said that he thought you may not have had time for your own breakfast, ma'am. So he has ordered this for you. I'll leave it here by the window and you can help yourself to what you like on it.' She dipped a polite curtsey and left.

Agatha lifted the silver cover up and saw a full cooked breakfast underneath on a porcelain plate.

'Blimey, lass, I'm in heaven!' Both women laughed and between them ate every morsel offered and drank every drop of the juice and tea. They were like two children having a party until the coach arrived and once more they had to part.

As Agatha climbed sadly into the coach, Millie ran down the steps after her.

'Here, Mrs Kell.'

Agatha turned and saw the maid was holding out on an earthenware jar.

'What's this, lass?' Agatha asked suspiciously, but Millie merely smiled at her.

'It's ointment for them hands of yours. You put a layer on every night and let it work on them whilst you sleep.'

She pushed it at her until Agatha took it.

Agatha looked at the long window of the morning room and saw a tall figure looking out.

'Take it, woman. It's a well-meant gift.'

'But why?' Agatha asked, unused to such generous gestures and deeply aware how much her hands pained her.

'Because your hands need it and it will help. No other reason. Now the coach will be sent for you on Friday at ten o'clock. If you want to see her in between you'll have to come yourself. Your old clothes are in the coach, but only come in these clean ones.'

Agatha hugged the jar to her and sniffed the air. 'Friday at ten. Tell him . . . tell him . . . he has my thanks.' She quickly got into the carriage and closed the door. Millie stepped back and waved at her before she ran up the Hall steps.

Agatha wondered what was at the bottom of it. No rich man was so kind to poor folk. It just wasn't done. What her Bill would make of it she dreaded to think. He was proud and stubborn and he didn't care for the incomers. They were changing the town and getting in the way of trade. Things were becoming more difficult and now they had her Georgie.

Agatha had seen how well tended she was and how she suited the surroundings so well. She wouldn't stand in the way. The girl was where she always had dreamed that her daughter belonged.

Even though she knew one day the lass would have to return to her humble home, it may give her some way of finding a better life.

She chuckled to herself as she lifted the wax paper and sniffed the sweet-smelling ointment. Perhaps that man in the stupid uniform would fall for her beautiful daughter. Then he'd have to call her Ma. She rubbed some of the ointment into her sore hands and felt a gentle feeling of relief spread. Impressed, she covered it back up.

She'd better keep it out of sight. If Bill smelt it, he might eat the stuff. She laughed and enjoyed her journey home in a fine carriage, wearing a clean dress and with boots that didn't pinch her. It was real and on Friday she'd do it all again.

4

By the time the coach arrived back in Scarbeck, Agatha had become quite used to the feel of her new attire. She watched the coach leave. The man in the stupid uniform looked down on her as he turned the carriage around. She realised it was not just in a physical sense of the word that he did so, but she held her head high and walked into town by The Angel Inn. She heard a whoop and a howl behind her and turned around to see her Bill sitting atop the low stone wall that tried to protect the inn from the sand being blown in, or the sea, to little avail.

'Hey, fancy a tumble in the dunes? Don't tell the missus, though, will yer?' He sucked on his pipe and walked over to him, her Bill. 'Hell's-bells, now I'm done for, it is the missus!' He feigned fear and she clipped the back of his shoulder.

'You are a fool. Have you caught any dinner today? If yer don't go out and get them, the fish won't come to you, yer know. They ain't no such thing as a suicidal fish.' She looked at him in despair.

He wrapped his arms around her and gave her a kiss. 'Yer look ten years younger. Only about fifty now!' He laughed at his own sarcastic joke; she was many years younger than that.

'Cheeky blighter!' She clipped him on the arm. He'd been at the inn all morning and hadn't been out in the boat at all. Any guilt she had felt for eating the fine food up at the Hall was soon put to rest because she knew how feeble her dinner would be. 'Where's that no good son of ours? Still in there, I bet!'

She stormed inside The Angel, heads turning her way. 'My, aren't we posh — one minute ridin' around in fine carriages, the other wearing a new frock and yer hair up in a bun. Soon you'll be goin' over to The Swan, too good for the likes of us workin' folk.' The voice that rang out was that of her own flesh and blood, her son, Daniel, and he had young Sally on his knee, a tankard in his hand.

'What workin' folk? I don't see no-one workin' where I'm lookin' '. She stared at him. He stood up. Sally slipped off his knee and staggered to prevent herself from sprawling on the floor.

'So yer go swannin' off to the gentry and come back screamin' at yer son! Have yer no respect, woman? We haven't gone out today 'cos we saw a woman before we set sail — you! So it's your fault, woman. Yer know our ways. Now did yer bring back any food from the kitchens or just steal a dress.'

He stood before her and Agatha had to suppress the urge to hit him hard. He was a big lad and they both knew he would swipe her back if she did. His father was weak and he was her only son, and she dearly wished he would go away, not Georgie, but her own son, Dan. He'd 'gone bad' since mixing with Conner and his gang.

They were building the new homes, but they also stole and spent much time drunk at night. They had taken over The Angel each evening and no-one complained as they fed them with news of the Carters' plans and gave the inn much needed income as it had to compete now with The Goose.

'Yes, yer sister had woken up, but is not coming home yet. She'll be touched that you asked after her.' Agatha turned around and stormed out of the inn, in disgust. He followed her and she passed Bill and made her way towards their cottage, carrying the bundle that was her own clothes.

'Ma!' Daniel shouted after her. 'There's no need to be like that, of course I want to know how Georgie is.'

She spun around and saw him standing with his hands at his side. For a moment he reminded her of the boy she had loved as a child.

'Then why didn't yer ask about the lass instead of insultin' yer ma, and in front of everyone? What are we to eat if all you two do is drink? How is it you have money for ale, but not for food? Tell me that, Dan, and begin with the name Connor O'Connor.' At the mention of the man's name he looked down, then out to sea, but not at his ma. He came closer to her.

'I hate the sea. I loathe it . . . ' he whispered the words as they would have him laughed out of town by the old villagers.

'No, lad, yer scared of it and have been ever since your granda was taken by it when you were a mere nipper. But men have to rise above such fears, or spend their lives in hidin'.' She put a hand on his arm, imploring him to return to her like the son he used to be.

'So you think I'm a coward, eh?' he asked provocatively and she knew that he had gone back into his new persona — the one that appeared tough and hard. Yet, she had seen a fleeting glimpse of the youth that had been her son only a year previous. He still existed, but was buried deep inside him.

'So when will Lady Georgina return to help earn our keep, Ma?' He folded his arms in an arrogant manner and that was what did it with Agatha.

She had seen good women ruined by their men folk, lazy drunken good for nothings and she would not have it for her Georgie.

'She's not coming back for some time. She's broken a leg and can't walk on it. So you best start collecting the bait and gettin' fish with the women and children, Daniel, if yer not goin' out with the men.'

She snapped her reply through gritted teeth, quiet enough for only him to hear and that was when the maternal bond was broken.

He slapped her across the face. She saw the regret in his eyes the moment he realised what he had done, but she backed away.

Never had her man done that, never in her life, and yet he stood and watched and did not defend her. Others had seen. Her pride, like her love for her only son, was shattered. She stormed back up the road out of town. He looked at his father who walked back into the inn. He followed him, grabbing Sally as soon as he entered.

5

By the time Agatha reached the gates of Carlton Hall she was in quite a bad state. Her cheek stung, her heart pounded and she was breathing fast. What would she say? What could she say to a man of the gentry? He had told her to swallow her stupid pride. Well she would. She'd beg if she had to, sleep on the stable floor, work all day and night in the laundry for nothing, just to be near her Georgie. Surely he'd let her . . . he must. Agatha was desperate. Agatha was breathing heavily.

The gravity of what she had just done made her sag at the knees. She'd walked out on her man and her son, but she couldn't tolerate being struck and in front of Biddy Jones as well. It was more than her pride could take and she had already swallowed enough of that with letting her Georgie be taken over by this stranger. Everything had happened so quickly she was so confused.

William recognised the figure instantly as he set off down the long driveway on his precious horse, Titan. He was about to ride to the town to inspect the work that the builders' gang was doing on the new houses that he had personally designed. Next there would be a school, a small hospital and almshouse, a vast stabling block as he aimed to breed only the best racing stock and then he would expand the newly-built Swan Inn to take in guests, as the sea air would be an excellent attraction for those needing air and a respite from the city.

Mr Carter had plans for this area. It was, as yet, an undeveloped coastal town; that was about to change. He had just secured the track that led from the old town to the coach road to Newcastle. The locals did not like the 'incomers' as they had called them, and William was well informed about the townsfolks' views. He had a reliable source.

He would see to it that they were soon in the minority, because new money brought trade and opportunity. However, he was not pleased with the builders. True that the work they did was fine enough but, there was a troublemaker amongst them if ever he saw one. The Irish chap looked at him with what he presumed to be finely-disguised hatred.

It was possible that he may not like Englishmen and with good cause, but William refused to stand trial for the greed of all his fellow countrymen. He suspected that the man O'Connor was becoming involved with the smuggling trade and Carter did not want his estate crawling with revenue or customs men.

He wanted to build a secure future, a new life for him and Charlotte who would shortly be joining him. Then his world would be complete, without the interference of the rabble.

Looking at the crumpled figure of Agatha hunched against the wall, peering pathetically at him through the gates as he approached, he was not at all pleased, or touched. What the hell the woman was playing at he couldn't guess. Hadn't he been understanding and generous with the care of her reckless daughter?

He had even given her mother a decent dress and boots and sent her safely home in his carriage only to find her begging again at his door. What was she trying to do? He wondered if she was imbalanced in the mind. She clearly loved her pretty daughter, but was it to obsession? Or was she having some sort of breakdown? He had thought she was made of sterner stuff; fisher-women were known for their hardiness.

'Why ever did you walk all the way back here, woman?' he shouted as he rode up to the tall iron gates. Then his manner softened. She was purple in the face and gasping for breath. He dismounted straightaway and secured Titan's reins to the wrought iron. 'What ails you?'

He released the button at the neck of

her dress. 'Your daughter is safe here; you have my word on it. Whatever possessed you to walk all the way back here? You are no longer a young woman and that is a four mile walk.'

It was then he saw her face and realised that she had been attacked. The bruise on her cheek had started to show. He abhorred violence on women. He had seen too much of it, from slaves in far off lands to the loathsome sight of domestic violence in the home — his own childhood had been marred by it. Straightaway he supported her weight as he helped her through the open gates. 'Who attacked you?' He sounded angry; but it was not with her.

Agatha shook her head and gasped a few words. 'Oh, it was an accident,' she tried to dismiss it. 'I'm a clumsy old fool.'

'No, you are no fool and neither am I. Tell me the truth, woman, or I'll make you walk the whole way back to your hovel.' He stared into her eyes and was surprised to see a glimmer of humour there.

'You have a way with words, sir.' She tried to smile but the tears trickled out of the corner of her eyes and down her cheeks. 'It was me own son, Daniel. I can't and won't lie to you but me man, my own Bill . . . he stood there and watched. Not even coming to me aid. They're lazy and me lad's been influenced by that O'Connor. He's a hard nut if ever there was one.'

She shook her head and she looked up at the Hall. 'Oh, I didn't know what to do, sir. I had no plan to be more of a burden to yer than our lass already is, but I couldn't stay there.' She sniffed the air and tried to compose herself.

She took in a deep breath, coughed slightly and with great effort said, 'I'll work for nothin' in the laundry if you'll let me stay here. Sleep on the scullery floor and no moanin', not about a jot. You have me word on it.'

The woman was struggling with her pride and he could sense her desperation. He shook his head; her skin had a colour to it that he recognised and did not like. Her heart was straining and not just for her daughter's company.

'No!' he said emphatically, and she immediately let out a gasp and sobbed.

'Please, sir!' she sniffed and gasped again, shallower this time. 'I've never begged for anyone to give me anythin' before . . . please.'

'No, you're not fit enough to work in the laundry or sleep on the floor. You shall have a servants' cot near the kitchens where it is warmer and, when you're rested and seem to be fit enough, you can do light duties helping the cook. There will be no remuneration whilst your daughter is receiving care, then we shall see what happens next.

'I will not have drunkenness, lewdness, or stealing in my home. Any one of them will have you instantly thrown beyond the gates and you shall not see your daughter again until she is fit to walk beyond them herself. You will not have your family visit here, except for the one who is in residence, and you will follow Cook's instructions regarding washing to the letter. Is that understood?' He looked at her. She was struggling to regain her composure.

'You're a good man, sir,' she said looking into his dark brown eyes.

He smiled, 'I doubt that, and I do not intend to start a hospital or a workhouse on the estate. Please tell me one more thing?'

'Yes, sir,' she said, as she hobbled along with him supporting her weight on one arm, in the other hand he held Titan's reins; the horse ambled lazily behind him.

'Are there any other female members of your family who I should know about?' He smiled at her kindly, appreciating that she was in quite an emotional state.

'No, sir.' She stopped to take her breath. It was shallow and frequent.

'Listen, Agatha. I am going to leave you here whilst I send Higgins with the gig. You are in no state to do anything. You will be made comfortable and you will rest for a few hours and not attempt to do anything at all. I think you have over-exerted yourself and have had quite a sharp shock. May I suggest that you try to keep your breath even and stop thinking about what has happened. You will be reunited with your daughter and when all this is sorted out, you will not have to return home to a woman beater unless you have a masochistic desire to do so.' He mounted the horse.

'I don't know what a massa . . . is, but I ain't goin' back . . . thanks.' She sat down on the ground and nodded at him. 'I don't want Georgie told about this,' she pointed to her cheek.

'Ma'am, how you explain that to your daughter is your affair. However, she is not expecting to see you until Friday, so let us stick to that arrangement. She is hardly likely to visit the kitchens in her state, and Millie shall not gossip.'

He headed back to the stables. It appeared that no matter how much he tried to turn away from the need to help people through his old work the more seemed to land on his doorstep — literally. It was beyond him to know how he would ever break free. But he could not stand by and see a woman abused.

6

Georgina had been lying on the bed for nearly a week. The food that she was brought regularly was healthy, fresh and good for her. She had tasted some meats and vegetables for the first time in her life. Even though she was a humble girl, her tray was laid out as if she was a lady.

Her routine was closely supervised by Millie. She had been taught how to groom herself properly and spend time looking after her long dark hair. Millie was fun and made excellent company when she could spare the time to be with her, but between those times there were long empty hours spent deep in thought. Sometimes she would see Carter riding his horse across the estate. Both, she mused, were handsome beasts and she longed to join them.

She had had to put up with many an embarrassing moment concerning her toilet, but Millie was a reliable and fine nurse who was discretion itself. She had only seen Mister Carter once in her room, for that was how she had started to think of it, since he initially examined her. She still blushed at the thought, but knew that it was her own stupidity which had nearly made her a cripple.

This way she was growing stronger, both with the rest, which was helping her leg to mend, and she was eating better than she ever had. Her complexion was rosy and other than the ache in her limb, she felt fine — but bored. How she would adjust to her old bland diet she tried not to think about.

She thought about her mother many times. Funny, she had realised that she had not given hardly any time to her brother and father. Then she had the long periods of contemplation and had come to the conclusion that they were either out at sea a lot or more often than not, down at the inn. They'd stumbled in late almost every night. She had hardly seen them. Her brother was moody by nature, and of late he had become increasingly so. Her father seemed to be resigned to his life — or, as Georgie had come to regard it, as a mere existence.

Staring at a window with such a view had become too much for her; she wanted to see more. Georgina could not remember the last time she had lain in bed so long. Slowly, gingerly, she inched her body slightly to the right.

She had decided that if, she reasoned, she placed her good leg on the floor then she would be able to support her weight and hop carefully over to the window seat. Then she would lift her leg up to the cushion and rest it there.

Georgina placed her foot on the ground and grimaced as she tried to slide her left leg into position. Suddenly she was not so sure that this was such a good idea. A pain shot up her leg like an arrow. She winced and stopped herself from screaming out loud.

Georgina precariously balanced on one leg, with her other leg aching as she rested it on the edge of the bed. She placed her hand on the bedside table. Unfortunately, she had not realised that it was not a solid piece of furniture and as she leaned on it with her weight, it moved. Georgina had nowhere to go other than straight down to the floor. She heard the door open as she teetered on the bed edge then started to slip and cried out for help, 'Millie!'

Two strong arms supported her weight under her armpits and pulled her to her feet.

'I thought I'd really done it that time!' she exclaimed, and laughed until she took her eyes off her feet and stared at the strong chest in front of her. In his boots, breeches and shirt, Mr Carter was standing holding her in his muscular arms. She looked up at him, the guilt of a child filled her, and she had been caught, literally and, fortunately for her, in the act of disobeying his orders. Her hair flowed loosely over her shoulders.

'I was bored,' she said, unable to move, and shamefully reluctant to, 'I was trying to sit on the window seat for a change of view . . . sir,' Georgina added as she admired his strong dark features. She offered her feeble explanation of why she had nearly undone a whole week's worth of healing.

'Do I need to tell you that you are a fool?' he said softly to her.

'I suppose I deserve that title. But I've never been still so long in my whole life.' She smiled at him. Georgina thought she should be scared of him but she wasn't. There was something both comforting and exciting about him.

'Well, that will soon change. You shall have some entertainment. Can you read?' he asked.

She flushed deeply, not with embarrassment but in anger. 'Of course I can read!' she snapped back.

'Lady, there is no 'of course' about it. You come from a poor background. Tell me then, if you can, how can you?' He was still holding her close to him. She could feel his body against hers, only his shirt and the material of her nightgown separated their flesh. She wondered if he was aware of how close they were to being together?

'Because, Mr Carter, I helped Reverend Cane. I taught Sunday School and helped him to keep his records.' She looked away and changed the subject quickly. 'So what entertainment do you suggest I partake in . . . ? Charades?' She smiled cheekily at him and was surprised when he smiled back at her.

'No, nothing so energetic. I shall bring some books up from the library and you shall be able to read them and broaden your mind. Then in a few days we will see about you learning to walk with the use of sticks. For now though, it is back off to bed.' Gently he lowered her and lifted each leg carefully back in place.

Then he sat in the chair by the bed and asked her lots of questions about the characters she had grown up with in town, including her family, her brother and her home. She was so happy to have some company that she regaled him with witty stories of her past misdemeanours and the customs and habits of the villagers, which she herself found quite bizarre at times.

It was when she asked him about where he had come from and his own life, that he realised the time had flown by. He promised he would come back with the books later, and she said she would look forward to it. He bent over the bed as he stood up and, as automatic as breathing, he placed a kiss on her forehead and said, 'Take no more risks, Miss Georgina, you have too much life left in you to damage yourself now.'

'Yes, sir,' she answered, and smiled at him. He had taken two full steps away before the realisation of what he had just done in that casual gesture dawned on him.

He stopped in the middle of the room, straightened his broad shoulders, glanced back at her, with his cheeks slightly flushed. William did not say a word. She held his gaze, not smiling, not joking, but silently understanding that there was something happening between them. An attraction, but they were, socially, worlds apart. Georgina looked out of the window towards the distant sea where her 'hovel', as he referred to it, was. He did not say a word to her, but left as quietly as he had entered.

William ran down the stairs, rebuking himself sternly. What was he thinking of? This woman, this girl, was his patient. Since when did he kiss, no matter how innocently, a patient? Yet it had felt so right. Deeply inside him, he had meant it and had wanted to caress her in a very different way.

Once at the bottom of the stairs, he decided he had better check on Agatha as he had no compunction to kiss her. He was about to enter the kitchens, something he barely ever did. This was the servants' domain, but these were strange times. Life was changing daily; he stopped before entering to straighten himself, forgetting he had not replaced his waistcoat.

'Listen, Kell, you speak of a word of what you see down here to 'is lordship up there and you best not close yer eyes at night. There'll be nowhere you'll be able to hide this side of Hull.'

He recognised the cook's voice instantly. Mrs Crabtree was threatening the woman she was supposed to be nurturing.

She continued, 'You be careful of what you say and to that incomer, Millie. She's 'is spy and I should think a lot more besides!' Her voice rose a little with indignation.

'All I said was, he seems a decent chap to me. He has treated our Georgie real good, and me, and it doesn't seem right that he should be cheated when he already gives help freely, Miss Crabtree.' Agatha was keeping her voice level and low.

'Aye, she's a pretty lass, your Georgie is. I wonder why he'd keep her up there and dump you down here, eh? Besides, you're no-one to talk about morals when yer walk out on yer husband and son. Shameful, if you ask me, that's what yer are.' She slammed a wooden spoon down on the table.

William had quietly come into Agatha's vision as he leaned against the stone archway.

'I wouldn't say any more, Mrs Crabtree, if I was you,' Agatha said quietly.

'Threatening me now, is it? You've a nerve.' The woman was incensed.

'No, warnin' yer.'

'Mrs Crabtree, I think you and I need to have a talk in my study. Agatha, see to your daughter's soup. Then sit in the hall and await my summons.'

Mrs Crabtree went white. The wooden spoon fell from her hand and she started blithering.

'My study!' Mr Carter shouted and the woman dipped a curtsey and ran out of the room, not before shooting a look of pure hatred in Agatha's direction.

7

Agatha waited outside Mr Carter's room for over an hour. She fidgeted and shuffled nervously on the seat. However, she could not hear anything of what was being said behind the locked doors. Eventually they were opened and Millie was summoned inside. Moments later she ran out into the main hallway towards the servants' corridor which led down to the kitchens.

After more long moments, Agatha heard the girl's returning footsteps as she ran along the stone-flagged passage and then saw her as she appeared at the narrow doorway carrying some papers. She adjusted her bonnet before walking at a fast pace across the polished marble hallway disappearing inside the study for another hour or so.

Agatha did not dare move from

where she had been told to sit but her mouth was drying as she contemplated what her fate would be if she was linked with Mrs Crabtree's systematic pilfering of the master's food. She longed to run up the grand stair to the nursery to see Georgina and tell her everything. She'd believe her and no doubting.

The door finally opened again and Higgins was summoned. This time Millie stood in the open doorway. Agatha was going to ask her if she could go now but, before she said a word, Millie put a finger to her lips to silence her. Higgins entered, but was only there a moment before he ran out of the study, down the hallway fastening his jacket as he went.

Millie stepped outside shaking her head at Agatha and looking very flushed. Mister Carter appeared next. He walked out stiff backed, looking severely annoyed. He was followed by an emotional Mrs Crabtree. He moved towards the stairs, but Mrs Crabtree turned and, amazingly for a plump woman, ran out of the Hall leaving the large doors wide open and headed towards the woods at the side of the building. Mr Carter did not hesitate; he calmly went to his desk, retrieved a pistol and aimed it from the open window.

He fired a warning shot from the gun above her head. The woman screamed and threw her hands up in the air before falling to her knees on the moist grass. Benson ran out after her and promptly frog-marched her back to Mr Carter who was now standing a couple of feet from where Agatha was still sitting.

'Lock her up somewhere where she can not escape from. Higgins has gone to find a militiaman. They will arrest her in the morning and take her to the lockup at Gorebeck.'

Mrs Crabtree begged for a second chance. He turned on his heel and totally ignored the woman's pleas and protests. 'Agatha, come to my study, now!' He stormed back inside the mahogany panelled room and stood staring out of the tall window. He closed it securely just as he had another chapter in his life. The woman would no doubt hang unless he intervened, then she may be transported. He would decide in the morning; he was too angry at the moment.

Agatha followed him inside the room and closed the door behind them. She stood there and waited for him to speak. He seemed to be breathing deeply with his hands held firmly behind his back.

'People will never cease to amaze me, or disappoint me. You take a soul into your home, train them up to be something they could never have been on their own, trust them and what do they do in return?' He turned around and faced her. 'They steal from you, that's what they do. Even when you have treated them fairly, paid and fed them well. I will not tolerate that kind of behaviour in my own home!' He was very angry.

'Sir, you don't know her kind well enough. She sees opportunities in everythin' you've done for her, not kindness. I'm sorry, you deserved better — respect, but we're not all like that.'

'If I hadn't heard you stand firm for my character, Agatha, you would be with her right now, no matter what Georgina thought about it. However, you did and said what was right. I, therefore, shall offer you the trial place as my cook.'

Agatha's eyes opened wide. She was obviously surprised and delighted at the offer.

'You will be given training and will be expected to keep records — can you do that?' He looked at her as her expression changed and she studied the floor for a moment.

'No, that I can't. I never have had need to know letters or the opportunity to learn.' She paused for a moment. 'She's a good lass. Georgie has never done nothin' that's wrong, knowingly. But I didn't have time to learn off her and she's the one with the looks and brains. I'm from simple stock, but my Georgie can use those skills to help me. I could tell her what to write down.'

She raised her head and her eyes seemed to be full of hope. 'We make a good team and you'd get two for one.'

'Very well, you have just inherited your predecessor's dresses and uniform. I maintain high standards here. I demand cleanliness not sloppiness, the very best service and well-cooked food. You will be given a month to come up to my expectations. If you succeed then you will be paid the same wage as that woman was. Do you accept the offer and the challenge?'

'Yes, Mister Carter. Can I decide where to order the supplies from then, as I don't think you're getting the best produce that you could? I may not be able to write, but I know when a chicken or an egg is fresh and where to get the best catch of fish at what price and from which boats. I can fight for a fair deal and I'm not easily hood-winked.'

Agatha stopped for breath obviously desperate to have the best chance of success.

He stared at her for a moment. 'Tell me, Agatha, does she have a young man?' He was looking down at some papers on his desk.

'Old Crabtree, she was married but he disappeared at sea. Her sons work in town but they're as greedy as she is . . . ' Agatha said in an incredulous voice.

'No, not her! I was referring to your daughter.'

'No, she's too good to be stuck with the likes of Jeb and Seth Crabtree. Good workin' lads that they is, but they isn't what you call a challenge for her. They'd shorten her life by killin' off her spirit.'

'Good, because I won't stand for anything of that nature in my home either. This Jeb had better wait for her to return to the town. If indeed she does. It rather looks as if I have not only found myself a new cook, but I shall see for myself how neat your daughter's writing is and perhaps she will be able to repay my hospitality once she is well. Now, find Millie and she will show you the ropes.' He looked up to find that the woman was still staring at him. 'Was there something else?'

'No, sir, I was just daydreaming, beggin' yer pardon.' She dipped an ungraceful curtsey and walked to the door.

'One other thing, Agatha . . . ' he waited until she faced him. 'Don't let me or yourself down. Opportunities like this do not happen often in a lifetime. You have seen what happens when one is abused.'

'Aye, I know that, lad, and I won't let anyone down, especially my Georgie.' She winked at him and smiled.

He raised an eyebrow at her and she realised what she had just said and done.

'Sorry, sir, I mean.' She shut the door quickly behind her and he smiled to himself. He liked her spirit, but moreover he liked the fire he saw in her daughter's eyes.

William swung his chair around and looked out across his vast estate. He had come from a worse situation than they had, but that he knew, and they didn't. He was a *sir* to them, and they were bound by his rank and their lack of it.

William was a free man. From the street where he was born he had made his own luck, been educated with the sons of gentry, sailed the seas and returned home. That had been his biggest mistake.

He had tried to help the people of his roots — the miners, and it had nearly cost him everything he had built up.

However, with his reputation restored and his wealth safely invested he made his own rules and chose his own friends very carefully. Crabtree had never fooled him. He knew her kind, stupidly blind by greed, but he had no better choice for a cook until he saw Agatha — a loving mother and victim of the brute of her son. He hoped she rose to the challenge. He would build his fortress, and man it with soldiers who he could trust, like Millie, Higgins and Benson.

Then he would find the woman he wished to share it with who could be a friend to his niece, Charlotte, who would arrive shortly. Only a few more weeks and they would be together again. He could not wait; everything he did, everything he built was for her.

He thought for a moment about her dear mother, her delicate manner and gentle eyes and his heart felt heavy. How he had failed her in her time of need. Memories of his own wife returned to him; despite all his training, all his struggling, the years of being bullied by the other boys as he tried to learn, he had succeeded despite them all, yet when it mattered the most and he had had Emma's life in his hands, he had seen it slip away unable to help her or hold on to it.

The memory alone still pained him. It had nearly broken his own spirit, confidence destroyed. Yet, here he was ministering to a young woman who was the opposite of his Emma. Georgina was feisty, strong and a fighter. Charlotte was like a daughter to him; the one who he should have had with Emma and not the result of a violation of a vulnerable young girl. But what would his Charlotte make of Georgina? Time alone would tell.

Meanwhile, he had decided the woman, Crabtree, should set sail to a far off land. He had no wish to be the reason for an unnecessary death. He would request that she be transported. She was hard and they needed her kind in the new land, Australia.

8

Weeks passed by and Georgina was enjoying reading *the master's* books. She laughed when she thought of him like that, because it conjured up images of a stern Lord of the land. Although he tried hard to adopt an authoritative stance as he went about his daily business, when he relaxed with her, as he frequently visited her in her room, he was easy in his manner.

Each time he came he brought her new books to read and took the ones she had read away with him. They would discuss what she had learned, from life issues, to the new ideas and thoughts about the world. Some even dared to question the word of the Bible, although he said it was good to be aware of these issues and opinions it did not mean that one had to follow their line of thought. Know your enemy, he'd say calmly and smile.

Many things were new to her. She learned how the body is structured and was fascinated by the drawings that he showed her. There was more under her skin than she had imagined and he had obviously studied it in detail. He even explained where her leg had been injured and what he had done to strengthen it and how the muscles would need exercising to support her weight, before the splint could be removed.

But their conversations always ended abruptly once she turned the topic and her questions on him and his illusive past. She knew very little about Mr William Philip Carter himself. When she asked about his own home, where he grew up, it was a door that appeared to close all conversations.

Her food had changed slightly, but her mother's skill as cook was improving. She had found out from Millie that Agatha was now the official cook after the very first meal she had prepared for her. It had been mackerel prepared in her favourite way, a little spicy and served with freshly-baked bread. Now mother and daughter saw each other at least once in every day. It was a perfect situation. Georgina's life was the happiest she had ever known it to be.

'Georgina, today you will be dressed when I call for you in one hour and you will be helped downstairs where I have a surprise waiting for you.' As usual William had entered her room with only a cursory knock as he walked in. She was washed and her hair brushed out and Georgina was as usual sitting on the bed with her leg supported on the stool.

'A surprise? Are you going to give me a clue as to what it is?' She beamed a smile at him as he walked around the bed and stood in front of her.

He knelt down and examined her leg splints. 'Now, put your foot on the floor. Don't pretend you have not tried it already.'

He slipped the silk slippers on to her

feet. Feet which were now soft and pink like her hands. Georgie tried not think about returning to her work catching flithers and mending nets or scrubbing the pots in the sink.

She had no idea how she and mother would return to the life in the town. They would be regarded as incomers themselves it would be so long since they had lived there, and they both were learning so much more now.

Georgina had not been told about Daniel attacking her mother or that Agatha had walked away from her husband and was the shame of the town; her name spoken as if she were the devil incarnate. Nor was she aware that her own name had been dragged through the dirt, too. It was rumoured that she had become the master's concubine. Not even Agatha was aware as to the depth of the resentment being brewed against them by a jealous Jeb, and a defiant Daniel. If Bill knew, he was unaware of it as now he was in a permanent drunken stupor.

'Rest your weight on me and stand up.' William moved the footstool out of the way and let her place her arms around his neck. He stood up to his full height and she straightened herself as he did. It was easier to do it this way with Millie because they were of the same height. However, with William they were unequal and she found herself resting against his chest.

He placed his hands on her sides and she felt his strength holding her safely, her body supported by his strong hands. He bent his head down to hers.

'I can't walk anywhere.' She was laughing. 'We appear to be too close,' she whispered.

'Indeed, we are, pleasant isn't it?' he replied, and kissed her briefly on the mouth.

She found herself responding to him, his grip on her changing as his hand slipped around her back and embraced her to him. Her hands caressed the back of his neck, her fingers exploring the thickness of his hair. What started as another innocent kiss grew in passion. Her body responded to his.

Georgina was quite overcome. She had never felt so vulnerable, so alive and so willing to cross the boundaries of common decency that had already been pushed back further than was acceptable by society. He threw his head back and stared up at the ceiling for a moment holding her tightly to him.

She released her hands from his neck, and rested them on his shoulders in order to steady herself. Her head rested on his chest, he breathed deeply.

'Whatever was I thinking of?' he said and stroked her hair with one hand. 'I apologise, I took advantage of you and I am disgusted by my own behaviour.'

'Don't be,' she said simply, as she reluctantly lifted her head and stood precariously on her own feet, 'Now, are you going to walk me to that chair or do I do it myself?'

He linked his arm in hers and she leaned on him until she was seated in the chair by the long window. She sat down and looked up at him, admiring everything she saw. He appeared to be looking at her as if he was miles away in his thoughts.

'Now then, here's yer breakfast tray and so nice it is that I thought I would bring it up myself.'

Agatha's voice surprised them both. Neither had heard her enter. Georgina was just relieved that she had not arrived a few moments before.

He took a good few steps back towards the doorway. 'Millie will be in to dress you in a moment and then you'll be taken downstairs. I shall see you there.' He left them, and Georgina tucked into the food eagerly.

Her spirits were high, so was her colour. Her mother stood there with arms folded glaring at her daughter. At first Georgina was not aware of it, but then as she took a sip of fresh milk she looked up and saw her mother's piercing eyes.

'What's wrong, Ma?' Georgie asked.

'That's what I want you to tell me. Is that man taking advantage of you? He comes in here and you next to naked, it's not right!' She folded her arms in front of her as she spoke.

'I'm nowhere near naked. This nightdress is almost as thick as sail cloth!' Georgina replied exaggerating, but determined to defend herself and allay her mother's fears. Her mother had seen them embrace, she was sure of that. Georgie was also sure that she didn't want him to stop and that she was falling in love with him.

9

Georgina longed to walk properly again, but dreaded the day she no longer had a reason to stay within this man's home. She would never be able to settle back to her old life, she wanted more; she wanted Mr William Philip Carter and what tore her heart apart was knowing that she couldn't have him. His kind was beyond her reach.

'You take care, girl. You let a man like that take liberties and there will be no holding him back. He has hooked you, girl, and soon he'll haul you in. I ain't goin' to stand by and watch whilst he fillets yer!' Agatha's voice rose slightly as she spoke.

'Ma! Wash your mouth out. What do yer think I am?' Georgina was appalled that her mother should speak to her in such a fashion. She knew from Sally what men did to women, but the girl had never explained the emotions involved within the act to her. Georgina wondered for a moment if they were the same for everyone.

'No, lass, you watch yersel'. We're here at his invitation. Both of us at his mercy, you take care how far you go, become the hook not the catch!' Agatha pointed to her tray. 'I didn't make that for you to let it go cold.'

'I've lost my appetite,' Georgie said defiantly.

'Then find it, now!' Her arms were folded again.

Georgina started to eat as Millie arrived all bright and full of chat as always. Agatha left, but not without one last penetrating stare at her daughter who tried to turn her head the other way as if it was water off a duck's back, but it wasn't and they both knew it. Georgina was in danger of giving in to body and heart, but it was her head that needed to regain control.

An hour later and she had been changed and helped down the stairs to the grand hallway. There she was presented with a pair of crutches and she precariously took her first unaided steps. Agatha, Millie and William looked on with Higgins and Benson standing behind her in case she fell or faltered, but Georgina didn't.

She was delighted to see the open outside door, the steps and the coach ready on the drive. She made her way to the doors and breathed fresh air, staring out across the vast estates.

'This is truly a beautiful place,' she said not realising that William was by her side.

'Yes, it is,' he answered confidently. 'Now, we'll help you. I do not think you should tackle stairs just yet.' She was carefully lifted down them by Higgins and Benson. They linked their strong arms under hers and she giggled like a happy child as they lifted her up and she felt as though she floated over the steps as they took her down to the carriage. The step was unrolled and she was helped inside.

William followed bringing the crutches with him. The door was shut and they moved off.

'Where are we going, sir?' she asked, feeling uneasy. This was exciting and unexpected, but she had not left the nursery rooms since arriving at the Hall some weeks before. It was the place she felt safe.

Now, dressed in fine clothes, sitting opposite William in the confined space of the carriage she felt shy, more than she had in the room. It was as though here the reality of their situation, the differences between them, was more stark. Also, her own reality was nearer.

'Where are you taking me?' she asked nervously.

'For a ride out. You have been pent up in that room for far too long. It is time you saw the sea and breathed deeply again. Besides, there is something I wish to discuss with you.' He smiled at her, and she looked at him, her heart racing.

Her hopes were raised. Did he feel

about her the same way as she did about him?

'What, sir?' she asked, trying not to sound too eager.

'Not here, when we stop. For now, just enjoy the view.'

The coach took them along the road until it turned off towards the coast along a lesser track to a small cottage. Higgins climbed down and opened the door. With some effort, Georgie was helped out.

'What is this place?' Georgina asked as she looked at the well-kept cottage and tended garden.

'This is my haven, and was for a time my home. Come inside, there is someone I want you to meet.' He opened the door for her and Georgie's heart sank.

Inside, a young girl was standing by a lace-covered table. She was slender, slightly taller than Georgina and, she presumed, approximately two years younger. He walked over to her, wrapped his arms around her and gave her a big hug. The same arms had wrapped themselves tantalisingly around her own flimsily clad body that very morning and held her so close to him. Georgie stared at them, leaning on her crutches not able to speak a word.

William turned to her. 'This is my dear Charlotte, my . . . '

Georgina could not help herself. Perhaps it was the sea air, the journey or being upright after lying down so long, but she wavered and teetered before falling. It was Higgins who caught her and rested her in a chair by the fire.

She came back to consciousness once more and was given a sip of water.

'I'm sorry, I don't know what came over me. I . . . ' Georgina was quite flustered. If she had two good legs she would have run out the door along the coast to the gill and hidden amongst the trees. All her hopes and aspirations were dashed. The girl was pretty and wore such a fine silk dress.

'Calm yourself, Miss Georgina. You

merely had a blackout. I should have insisted that you sat down when we arrived, but I was so anxious for you to meet Charlotte I forgot myself. This is my niece, and friend, Miss Charlotte Judith Armitage. She has recently arrived from Edinburgh and will be living at the Hall from now on, until she is wed. This cottage belonged to her aunt, my elder sister who has now graciously agreed to move into my estate.'

The girl who had the delicate face and complexion of a real lady smiled at Georgina, a little timidly. She was younger than Georgie had first thought, but obviously a tall girl.

'I'm pleased to meet you,' she said shyly, and offered Georgina her gloved hand.

Georgina shook it gently not knowing quite how to respond to the gesture. 'And . . . I you.'

'Where is Henrietta?' William asked.

The girl opened her mouth to speak when a voice resounded from the doorway, 'She is here! Dismiss your man, William.'

William nodded at Higgins who swiftly made himself scarce. Henrietta stood no more than five feet tall, dressed from head to toe in a dark brown dress and bonnet. Her eyes were direct and her hair tied back severely upon her head, not one hair daring to break free. Once the door behind her was closed she looked at Georgina who was, she guessed, sitting in the lady's chair.

'So this is the cripple,' she said in an ungracious tone.

'This is Miss Georgina. She is to be a companion for Charlotte. She is well read and very astute. I am sure they will pass many a fine hour together whilst she convalesces from her unfortunate accident.' He looked fondly on at the woman who seemed a match for him or any street fighter, Georgie guessed.

'Charlotte, go and sit in the coach, dear, I shall be there shortly.'

Charlotte smiled at William, collected

her reticule and left them. Again Henrietta closed the door.

'Is this the Kell girl?' she asked him. Her cheeks flushed and William's countenance changed. He looked at her seriously.

'What of it? Do you know her?' William asked, obviously surprised that she should know the name.

'Know her? No we have not had the pleasure, but I know about her. I visit the post you know and the dress-maker in the village and attend church regularly — unlike your good self. She and her mother are the talk of the area. Surely, you must have heard the gossip?' Henrietta's eyes narrowed and she looked from one to the other, assessing them.

Georgina returned her stare defiantly. 'What gossip?'

'What gossip?' William repeated, a half smile crossing his face.

'Well, according to the locals, the mother walks out on her own drunken lout of a husband after being publicly struck by her own son. Then she takes refuge up at 'the big house' where 'the master',' she looked at William who dutifully bowed slightly to her, the woman sniffed reminding Georgie of Agatha, ' . . . has already established a relationship with the Kells' daughter. It is said that he is so infatuated with her that he never lets her out of his private rooms. Even to the point that he is bewitched by her and her ways!' Henrietta stopped and looked at Georgie, whose mouth had dropped open.

10

The woman watched as Georgina fumbled with her crutches to try and stand up. Henrietta ripped them from her grip. 'Sit down you little fool!' She gave the crutches to William who held them in one hand.

'My mother would never walk out on my family or stand for being struck by a man . . . particularly not our Daniel.' She looked up at William, who was staring at the empty hearth. 'Is it true?'

'I took Agatha in because your brother hit her and your father did nothing about it. Yes, that much is true.'

'Take me there, please. I must speak with them. They don't understand what has happened.' Georgina looked up at him but he merely shook his head.

'It is you who do not understand what has happened. Your mother was right to walk away from such louts and

I suggest that you never return. Your brother is heading for trouble and will not listen to reason; your father . . . is continually drunk. I'll have Higgins go and see if there is any chance of sobering him up.'

Henrietta looked at her in disbelief. 'Did you not hear 'all' that I said, woman. You are named as no better than a harlot . . . well, perhaps slightly better as, instead of taking on all corners, you have planted your head on his pillow alone.' She pointed to her brother who merely lifted an eyebrow.

'Do you think I would take advantage of a woman in pain and distress, Hen?' he asked as he ruffled a hand through his hair.

'No, you wouldn't, but . . . has she taken advantage of you, my little brother?' Henrietta snapped back at him.

'Miss, I . . . '

'Mrs, but never mind that for now.' She looked at Georgie.

'We have done nothing improper.'

Georgie flushed deeply, trying not to dwell on what they had done. 'Mr Carter has helped me and for that I am grateful. People will always talk and they will be jealous. No matter what we say or do to deny this, nothing will appease their insatiable need for ruinous filth.' She looked up at William. 'I'm sorry that I have marred your reputation, sir.'

To her complete surprise both Henrietta and William looked at each other and laughed out loud.

'See, isn't she just as I described her in my letter, Hen?' William held his hand out to Georgie and helped her to stand up. 'Come, my captive maid. It is time I put you back in my castle,' he said smiling broadly at her.

'Have you no care for what they say about us?' Georgina asked, as she stood up.

'Not a jot!' he exclaimed, and winked at Henrietta.

'Not even you?' Georgina asked Henrietta.

'Oh, I care and I think he has underestimated the work there is to do with you, but I have decided to rise to the challenge.' She took the crutches and placed them under each of Georgie's arms.

'What challenge?' Georgina asked and met the woman's gaze equally.

'To make a silk stocking from a sow's ear!' was her curt reply. She opened the cottage door and they returned to an excited Charlotte who eagerly awaited the journey to the Hall.

11

Georgina stared out of the coach window as they travelled on the way back to the Hall. Her leg rested against William's as they sat side by side. He chatted to the two women animatedly. She saw the turning in the road for Scarbeck and looked down, over the open fields to the flat sands beyond the dunes.

Georgina could see The Angel Inn, and behind it the cobles going out, cutting through the breakers and heading out to sea on the waves. She didn't see *The Mermaid*, her father's coble. She'd know it anywhere as it had a red stripe on one side. Her father had never found the time, or made it, to finish the job and paint the other side to match.

'Could we drive down to the town, William? I think, perhaps, it is time that this girl saw her father again. Whatever else he is, he is her parent.' Henrietta looked pointedly at William, who shook his head.

'There will be a time when the visit is right to make. Now is not the time. We shall take Charlotte home and the two of you shall settle in. Millie is preparing your rooms. You shall have the old nursery to use as your own, and you, my dear sister, will have the suite next door. In that way you have your own privacy when required or you can join forces against me as you wish.' He winked at Charlotte.

'Is it full of toys still, or do you realise I have grown up in the last year?' Charlotte asked, and Georgina realised that despite her gentle appearance she was another strong character, from the confidence in her voice.

'I can see, my dear Charlotte, that you are a most mature young lady, so I have had the toys removed and in time you can choose how you would redecorate the rooms to your own preference. However, they are the lightest, airiest rooms in the Hall and one of my favourite views of the estate can be seen from the windows there. So you are being honoured, rather than patronised, by my turning them over to your care.'

'Then I am flattered to be placed in a nursery once more.' She smiled at him and looked at Georgie, who despite the pleasant expression on her face was wondering where that meant she would be staying from now on. One thought crossed her mind . . . the kitchens with her ma?

'So when does Miss Georgina see her home again, William?' Henrietta asked.

'When I think it is fit that she does so!' William's voice was firm and the slightly impish look in Henrietta's eyes disappeared. It was if the two had a way of communicating their intent without using many words.

Without giving though to what her question would sound like, Georgina asked, 'Where shall I be sleeping then?'

All eyes turned to him, and Henrietta raised a quizzical eyebrow.

'I would have thought that was obvious. Have not the tongues already wagged and declared it. You will be sleeping in my tower of course, until I let you out of it,' William answered, and winked at her. Henrietta and Charlotte laughed.

'You are a tease and a torment, Carter. Tell the poor child or else she will have nightmares about being thrown back to her hovel.' Henrietta gave his knee a light slap.

'It was my home! It may be a hovel to everyone else, but it was the place I was born and lived with my family,' Georgina answered sternly, but even her firmest voice appeared to amuse Henrietta.

'Your leg now needs to be strengthened. I want you to practise using those crutches, and for that it would be beneficial that you are moved to the ground floor. You need to be where you can walk easily. So you shall be sleeping downstairs. I have a room next to my study that I used as a bedroom when I was planning this estate and working on all the designs I had for it.

'I propose to move you in there; unless you would prefer to be amongst the noise of the kitchens with your mother. However, there would be little privacy and the conditions in the maids' rooms are far more cramped.

'The room I propose is perfectly situated and private. Of course you wouldn't dream of trying to go down the main steps to the hall and escaping without help, would you?'

He looked down at her and she saw Charlotte grin. They all appeared to have a friendly relaxed way about them. Georgie could see that they loved each other like she loved her own ma, but the difference was she had never felt that way with her own brother and father. Her home, her hovel, had been a place of hardship.

'Were you going to ask me about this proposition, sir, or do I not have any say in the matter at all?' Georgina asked him and saw he was slightly taken aback by her seemingly ungrateful attitude.

'Of course, Miss Georgina, I would not dream of presuming to force my charity and help upon you unwanted.' His voice was deliberately over pompous. 'Would you mind taking up residence in the annexe room to my study?' he asked her politely.

'No . . . I wouldn't,' she paused, and watched them all exchange surprised glances, then continued, 'I would be more than happy to accept your offer and apologise for the inconvenience I have caused. I thank you for your consideration and thoughtfulness.' She faced him and saw the relief in his eyes. Georgina realised he actually wanted her near him, and the thought warmed her.

They all laughed together.

'You, miss, are as much a tease as he is!' Henrietta exclaimed.

She placed her hand in his and

happily and openly sat nestling it until they entered the driveway to the Hall. Then he returned to his *master of the manor* roll and was extremely *proper* once more. Georgina was the last person to be helped out of the coach.

Agatha ran down the stairs to her. She seemed to be in quite a fluster. In fact, she was in such a flap with herself she could hardly get the words out of her mouth.

'Whatever is the matter with you, Agatha?' William asked.

'Perhaps, the young lady should go inside like,' she said, with the most artificial smile on her face that Georgina had ever seen. 'I mean, sorry to bluster in upon you like this. Of course the guests need to get to know the place after their journey.'

Henrietta assessed the situation immediately and took the woman's hint, ushering Charlotte up the steps to the Hall. 'We will speak later, William. Have your man send up the trunk, please.'

William nodded and they waited

until the two women were out of earshot.

'What has happened, Agatha?' William asked. It was obvious that he took the woman's unusual behaviour seriously.

'Trouble, sir. Big trouble,' Agatha gasped.

'Can you be more specific, woman?' William asked her impatiently.

'They've broken Crabtree out of the lock-up and word 'as it that her sons . . . ' she looked at Georgina, 'and mine, are getting the villagers all stirred up. They're up to no good, sir and I think it's you that they want.' She looked at him. 'Take it serious, lad. Your life's in danger. You'll need to watch yer back or it'll have a knife in it.' Agatha looked at him. 'I'm sorry for this trouble. It appears we have not brought you much luck for all your kindness.'

William let out a long slow breath. 'If they play dirty, Agatha, then so shall I. Come let us settle the ladies into their new home. Make them up a tray of your best culinary delights, Agatha and make it good because you now have my sister to please and her standards are very high. Then, I shall send Higgins and Stephens together to a friend I have in the mines.

'We shall see how they fare when they meet their match. Help Georgina back into the hall. I shall return by dinner. Please make yourself better acquainted with Charlotte, Georgina, I'm sure you will be the best of friends.'

He ran up the stairs three at a time and disappeared into the Hall.

'Ma, how bad is it?' Georgie asked, as she leaned against her mother.

'Well, they aim to get him, one way or another, and by God if they know I split on them I'm as good as dead too.' Agatha shook her head. ''Tis not a good day.'

'Why does Daniel have to spoil everything all the time? He was the one who got Pa so drunk and stopped him going out in the boat, like he used to. Oh, Ma. Now he's threatening our new life. You look better than you have in years. Your hands are mending and I

. . . and I . . . Oh, if only I had not broken this leg. I could sort our Daniel out and bring Pa to his senses.' Georgina looked at her mother who was shaking her head at her.

'Lass, if you hadn't run out in front of that man's horse, our Daniel could have turned on you at anytime. He's gone bad. If I'm honest he's always been that way, but I made excuses for him because he was me only son and I had hopes for him. Don't curse your leg or yer accident. You would never have known what life could have to offer you and . . . ' she moved her head next to Georgie's ear, 'You would never have met a man like that to fall in love with if you hadn't crossed his path the way yer did.'

Georgina opened her mouth to speak but her mother shook her head at her once more.

'Don't deny it, lass. If I were in your shoes I'd do the same. He's as fine as the horse he rides. What lass wouldn't want him?' Her mother smiled but

Georgie's eyes turned moist.

'But what's the point, Ma. He's a gentleman and he can do much better than me. Look at his own niece, she is a beauty and he loves her,' Georgina sniffed.

'Aye, he might love her as an uncle should love a niece, but he has eyes for you. Mr Carter is a man who fights for what he wants in life, and girl, if I know anythin' about men, I'd say he'll take on this fight because he wants you.'

'I'm being moved downstairs so that I can practice walking where there are no stairs,' Georgina explained, 'For no other reason Ma. He could have any fine lady — I have nothing to offer him.'

'Codswallop! He wants yer near him. He wants yer safe. Girl, he wants you!' She kissed Georgie on her cheek. 'And, lass, if yer know what's good for yer, you'll let him fight for you, and when he's made yer respectable, only then should he win his prize.' Agatha winked at her. 'That prize, the gift yer can give him is happiness. Love. That's the greatest gift of all that there is.'

Agatha helped Georgie up the stairs, and Georgie did not answer her, there was no need to.

Horses thundered down the drive as William, Higgins and the game keeper galloped along, each man carrying a rifle on his back.

12

Agatha did not take Georgina to her new room; instead she walked her slowly down the corridor towards the kitchens. She seemed to be almost excited, as if she could not wait to return to what was now her own domain.

'How did you find out all that information, Ma, when you're stuck up here away from the town's folk?' Georgina asked, as they made their way along the stone flagged floor at a steady pace.

'Yer best brace yourself, girl, for a big surprise, or should I say a skinny one . . . I've got a shock waitin' for yer by the fire.' Agatha smiled at her.

As they entered through the stone archway Georgina saw her father sitting on a stool by the warm fire. He was thin, thinner than he used to be, and looked as though he had been crying. A man, crying! The idea was far removed from any she had ever known. It was one of the things that wasn't done, unless a boat had gone down at sea and someone's son had died with it, then everyone had tears in their eyes — even the hardiest of sailors.

'Pa,' she said, 'I . . . ' she didn't know what to say. There was so much left unspoken, yet so little she could put into words.

He ran over to her, stooping and ringing his old hat in his hands. 'Georgie, yer look grand. I've missed yer, lass. I've wanted to come, but been too . . . '

'Drunk is the word yer lookin' for, Bill Kell!' Agatha snapped back at him.

'Oh, lass, don't be like that. I wanted to come here but it's so 'ard and after what happened I just didn't know what to do. I should've, I know.' He looked down, a broken man.

'More's the pity on yer then! Now, let the lass sit down before she falls on her face.'

'Georgina, lass, sit down here.' Her

father brought her a chair.

'How did you become so sober, Da?' she asked him, his hand wavering as he let go of the chair.

'I put out to sea and stayed in the boat for three whole days and nights with nothin' but water to drink.' He looked at Agatha. 'I was so ashamed of what I'd done, or not done, that I hid from folk, and drank only the water and ate nought. I came to my senses and will never drink another drop other than tea or water again, I swear . . . I miss yer, Aggie. I just don't want to be without yer.

'I'm sorry, lass. Please don't say you'll never have me back. I told her about Daniel and 'is plans to show yer I mean to put things back to rights. Yer've got to give me another chance, please?'

'I think I best leave you two to talk to each other in private,' Georgie said, and put her hand on the table to try to lever herself up again.

'You stay put. I've no need for privacy, nor time to think. I've lived with this lout all me life. He fathered me kids, both living and the dead ones and there were enough of them, God rest their souls. I love 'im. I always have but if yer want me back as a wife yer have to earn yer keep and my respect.

'Put yer boat out on the sea, catch the fish and stay away from our Dan and his 'new' friends. If yer found drunk just once more I'll not even look at yer in the street. But I ain't leavin' here. You prove to Mister Carter you are a reliable fisherman and see if he'll find a role for yer on the estate. That place we used to exist in is no home of mine, not any more.

'You let Dan have it. He deserves to be there on his own and rot in his own misdeeds. I can't believe that I would ever say such a thing about me own flesh and blood, but he nearly destroyed me family. If he is set on destroyin' 'isself then he can get on with it without draggin' us all down with him. Are yer clear on me feelings now, Bill Kell?'

'Aye, lass, I am and you'll not regret

it. I love yer woman. I shouldn't have to say it, but I will.' He kissed and embraced her, and Aggie slapped his back, but Georgie could tell she was a happy woman once more.

Her parents hadn't hugged like that in years and that was where Georgie had decided they had gone wrong. You could never have too many hugs, she thought, and remembered hers with William, and smiled as her being was swept by an excited feeling of warmth.

If only he was truly hers, she thought, then she remembered how he had ridden off with two men all armed with rifles. The warmth turned to cold as fear replaced contentment.

★ ★ ★

William galloped across the open fields to the edge of the moor where they rode on to the coast road and headed towards the bay town north of Whitby.

If his information was right then he would find the people he was seeking in the Jolly Sailor Inn, but he would have to be quick as he knew they sailed on the day after tomorrow. He may have to buy their services.

However, he was not beyond that. Not if it meant he would not have to watch over his shoulder for the rest of the days of his life. He had enough ghosts from the past to haunt him; he did not intend to harbour any more.

He saw the inn nestled in a sheltered spot on the edge of the moor at the top of the town's steep bank.

A track ran from its door down to the small fishing village below, itself being flanked by the treacherous cliffs and unrelenting open sea.

'Stephens, stay here and keep your eyes fixed on the roads. Both the coach one and the track.' The man nodded, and disappeared on to the moor unseen. He was army trained, a sniper, who was used to many a skirmish. Carter had picked his men very carefully. He had learned the value of true loyalty and friendship early in his life. A miner's life could depend on those very factors in the harsh reality of their underworld.

William had saved this man's life and that breeds the sort of loyalty you cannot buy. If he hadn't been accused of murder by the lying letch of a mine owner he would still be there, working amongst the people — his people.

The case had been dismissed, his honour, now tarnished with the dirt of the accusation of his misconduct, had been supposedly restored. But that very same owner had paid heftily for his slur, and as William's mother used to say, gold comes out of dirt, so William refused to be bitter, and started a life anew — again. But his confidence in his ability to use his medical training had, for a time, been rocked.

Had he been wrong in his diagnosis? The doubts had torn at him night and day until the truth had been disclosed. Even the thought that he knew he was good did not comfort him, because the man, his patient, had died when he knew he should have been cured. It had been Higgins who had discovered the truth of the affair.

The man had been passed a draft, an overdose, to rid the mine of a spokesman for the people, and frame his supporter, William, setting him up to take the fall. Or to be more precise, the drop, if he had been found negligent. And why? Because he challenged the morals and methods of the greedy mine owners, where profits were everything and humanity nothing.

They had caused the death of his own father and the extra toil and heartbreak had caused the early demise of his mother. William had risen from the ashes of his despair. A chance meeting had changed his life once again. He had returned the stolen purse of a man in Newcastle from a thieving pick-pocket even though he had become a street urchin himself. But that man had been a man of God. A wealthy one at that, and had seen the good within him.

William had discovered a benefactor,

and so his life and path changed forever, and through it all, he had promised his sister, Henrietta, that if she could survive the workhouse he would return for her and give her back her life. He had, by the grace of God. He had and had rescued her and her newborn daughter from a merciless life.

Hen had found a way to survive and Charlotte was the result, the illegitimate child of the overseer. Hen insisted on calling herself 'Mrs' for Charlotte was to believe her father was a poor man, with no shame attached to that, who died within the workhouse walls.

Charlotte was as beautiful in her fairness as Georgina was with her dark hair and features. No blame would be attached to them in his eyes for being born poor, nor to his dear sister, Hen, for doing what she had to, to survive. He realised how deeply he loved all three, which was why he would do all in his power to rid himself of this threat. But he was troubled by his over impulsive and improper behaviour towards Georgina.

He would have to take care not to use her situation to his advantage. Hopefully, once all the problems were resolved and her leg healed Georgina would realise how much he genuinely cared for her; no, that was not right and he knew it, he loved her. But first he had to deal with the rabble and make their future a secure one.

'Sir?' Jimmy the game-keeper's voice pulled him back from a world that existed so long ago, to the reality of his presence. The inn in front of him was quite busy. Music drifted out along with the bawdy calls of the inmates. 'We shall need to be careful,' he said as he dismounted and held his gun in his hand.

This, he was in no doubt, was the best way to go forward — the only way; unless he risked the noose himself, taking matters into his own hands, and that he would not do. He had too much to live for.

★ ★ ★

Georgina looked at her parents. It made her so happy to see them together again; it had been far too long since they had been a family. 'Let me speak to Daniel. He listens to me,' she pleaded with them.

Agatha waved a wooden spoon at her daughter. 'You'll do no such thing, lass. That sorry excuse for a youth don't listen to no-one anymore, unless he is called O'Connor. He will be the end of him, mark my words. Me own son gone to ruin!'

Agatha put the spoon down, shook her head and ruffled Bill's hair affectionately with her hand. 'I knew you'd come round. You always were slow to think things through but yer get there in the end, don't yer?'

'I'm sorry, Aggie . . . ' Bill started to fluster again. Georgie realised he was a weak man, worn down by life, but she loved him — because he was her father.

'Oh man, now stop yer blitherin'.

Move on in life and we'll all start afresh.' Agatha kissed his forehead but, as she straightened up, her eyes fell upon another familiar figure leaning against the stone archway.

'Well, well, well. There's more folk findin' their way to my door than The Angel Inn!' she declared, but there was no humour in her voice and her eyes were definitely alert. Georgie turned to face what was the cause of her mother's comments.

'Yeh, start afresh, man. Don't stand up on yer own two feet. Desert yer son. He don't fish, do he? He don't like the sea. He's a coward, isn't he, Ma? He ain't good enough for his precious sister, Georgina, the harlot of Carlton Hall!

'No, Da, you hide behind two women's skirts and before you know it you'll be wearin' one yerself then we'll all see who the coward is around here. One sow is old and past it and the other a strumpet and a cripple!' Daniel's voice, loud and charged with emotion echoed around the kitchen.

'Daniel!' Georgina looked at him. He appeared to be different — rough, unshaven, unwashed and hard, in a way she had never seen him before. It frightened and disturbed her. Would he attack them — like he had her ma? 'Think about what you are saying. Ma and Pa are back together, Daniel. We can be a family again.' He was staring directly at Agatha who had picked up a kitchen knife.

'Go on, use it, you stupid woman. Kill your one and only son. You hate me anyway. I dare yer to try it,' he taunted his mother.

'Daniel! In God's name tell me what has become of you. How can you stoop so low?' Georgina had stood up on her crutches.

'It's easy, sister. Just like entertainin' the master of the house.' He laughed at her mockingly.

With unexpected speed and force, Bill punched him so firmly on his jaw that Daniel didn't even see it coming.

He hit the floor and blacked out before the youth could move or dodge the punch.

'Da!' Georgina exclaimed, nearly losing her balance. Agatha steadied her then gave Bill the biggest hug she ever had in all their years of marriage.

'I knew yer had it in yer.' Her eyes were watering. 'Now help me lock the fool up in one of the store rooms. Hopefully, you'll have knocked some sense into his head. Oh man, I've waited a long time for this day.'

13

William entered the inn. The locals were already jittery; they had unwelcome guests amongst them drinking their ale. The landlord had refused to serve them at first, but then they had threatened him with arrest for standing between him and the Crown's business.

For they represented HM Navy and had the law of the land on their side. They were the pressgang. Ignoring the suspicious stares of the locals, he approached the officer in charge and offered to buy him a drink.

'Never say no to a friendly offer.' He glared at the faces turned to them and they soon looked back down at their drinks. 'There aren't too many about in this God forsaken place.'

A jug of ale was ordered and an extra to share between his band of men. 'So are you offering to join HM Navy, sir, or are you just looking for someone to drink with? You don't look the sort that is short of a shilling of his own. No need for the King's, eh?' The man was short and stout and not someone that he would trust or normally choose to sup with.

'I heard you need good strong men to serve our country. Ones with plenty of fight in them.' William looked directly at the man's beady eyes.

'You heard right, my friend. Don't suppose you have some you don't rightly need?' The man smiled, unshaven and with rotten teeth he looked none the better for it.

William lowered his voice. 'Yes, in a manner of speaking, I know where there are some rabble-rousers. They aim to break up my property and no doubt my skull if given the chance. I don't intend they should have that chance. The leader is Irish, a builder and strong as an ox, but troublesome.'

The man lowered his drink and stared at William. 'Where are they?' he asked, his eyes gleaming hopefully at the prospect of nabbing the men.

'Not here. Finish your ale and bring your men up onto the coast road and I will take you there. I'll give you three or four strong men and in return you take them to your ship and leave this village and Scarbeck alone. Do we have a deal, sir?'

The landlord looked over as he said these words.

'You let the local lad that you found and tied up in their stables return to his family here, and I will deliver these trouble makers into your arms.' William looked around as people waited for the officer's decision.

William had guessed that the fact these men were even sitting in the same inn as the impressment-men meant they were about to take their boy back forcibly, as soon as the gang stepped outside into the darkness of the night.

'Gibson,' the officer shouted after studying the hardened expressions upon the faces that watched him. 'Go and free the sprat, and we'll go catch us some mackerel.' The officer downed his drink, then faced William. 'You better not be trying to hoodwink me, boy, or I shall willingly put a hood over your head before you drop!' He snarled out his words and his stubbly face contorted with his menace. William knew his type, he'd seen them before, bullies in uniforms.

'I do not take kindly to threats, sir, particularly when there is no need.' William looked straight into his uncouth face.

'Men, finish up,' he shouted ordering them all outside.

William stood up and paid the innkeeper for the ale. 'It's on the house, sir.'

Moments later the young lad entered the inn. He looked as though he had put up a good fight for his face was bruised and his young skin cut. One of the men hugged him.

As William left they all looked at him and he knew he had at last won over the trust of the local fishermen. Now, all he had to do was to deliver on his promise, knowing though that the locals would not stand in his way. He was an 'incomer', but so were the men he was sacrificing to the pressgang, except for the lad, Daniel Kell.

His father wouldn't put up a fight for him, of that William was sure. Any man that could stand by and watch his own wife be struck by his son was not worth the ground he stood on.

Outside the men gathered. They were as good as hardened infantry, light on foot and used to walking miles. So the progress they made was far from slow. Under the cover of darkness and with stealth they approached The Angel Inn. William, Higgins and his gamekeeper had all dismounted a mile or so away from the town. Higgins led them across the marsh to the south of the town, keeping low as they traversed the dunes and crossed the flat sands towards the inn.

They clung to the shadows of the

beached cobles and crept around the inn below the level of the window's view. Waves broke noisily in the distance, crashing against the shore. Spray filled the air, tasting salty and fresh. The sound of the water's motion filled the air as the waves surged in the distance.

They waited until eventually a group looking for trouble left the inn. O'Connor led them. They headed up the road toward the Hall carrying heavy blackthorn clubs. William and the pressgang followed them, silently, until they were well away from the town and on the open road. It was then they struck.

First, confusing their prey by shouting orders and then surrounding the bemused group. It was made up of eight fully-trained men against five of the press. The odds seemed to favour O'Connor so he was brash, loud and threatening, but it was when the rifle shot rang out and splintered his club that the group split, leaving O'Connor with his two loyal henchmen.

The others disappeared over the marshland, they'd sobered up quick and would find their way back to their local hearths without further trouble.

'Drop yer clubs, lads. Don't do anythin' foolish, that yer might not live to regret!' The voice of the officer rang out.

O'Connor hesitated. 'You have no right to take us. We are here working men already. We work for the owner of the big estate. He wouldn't like it if yer left his houses half built, now would he, eh?' There was an air of arrogance in the tone of his voice.

'Somehow, I don't think so. Are you coming peaceably or do we have to use force?' Before O'Connor could answer, another shot rang out, this time shooting the ground between his feet.

O'Connor swore, and dropped the club. His men followed and they were tied firmly with their hands behind their backs, and walked on.

William stayed out of sight as did his

men. There was no joy for him in this. The men would be broken in spirit to remove their disruptive streak and if they survived that, then they had Napoleon's navy to deal with. But they had threatened him and his family.

Now, the people he cared about most in all the world were safe. But one thing surprised him, the youth, Daniel was not with them. So he had a loose end still running wild, and this saddened him, because he would have to deal with him, personally. But he would have to be very careful, because he was Georgina's brother.

She would hardly accept his forthcoming proposal if he caused injury or arrest to her wayward kin. He would propose to her once that her leg was healed and she no longer felt beholden to him. He did not want her gratitude, he wanted and needed her love.

William remounted Titan. He would have to think long and hard about the problem of Daniel, but not tonight. He stroked the horse's mane. Tonight, he thought, he should like to return to his study, and smiled to himself, knowing he would not be alone.

William returned to his home feeling very tired. He was fighting with his conscience but he was determined not to give in to it. He had done what was right and just. The men who were now going to serve in the war had abused his trust, taken his money — a fair wage, and still wanted to make trouble against what the men saw as English gentry.

Hatred was a vile emotion that William held no truck with. It destroyed lives. However, he reasoned that it was better that it destroyed their lives than his own one.

With renewed hope and anticipation, he knocked on the door behind the desk in his study. The room behind it was his little sanctuary. He had restored it first and from there he set about planning the conversion of the run-down Hall into its present form. There was no reply to his knock, therefore, he presumed she was already asleep.

The trip out in the fresh sea air must have tired her, he reasoned, so he slowly opened the door and peaked inside. The bed was made, the water to wash in was undisturbed on the side table, but there was no sign of Georgina or anything that would suggest she had been there at all.

'Where is she?' he muttered to himself, feelings of disappointment mingled with concern. He had longed to see her again and to reassure her that all would be well. Then the outstanding loose end of Daniel crossed his mind, and he felt fearful for her.

If the youth could hit his mother, what would he do with a sister who was reputed to have graced his bed? He clenched his fists trying to restrain the unexpected feelings of panic that were rising within him. The thought of Daniel laying a finger on Georgina made his blood boil.

He forced himself to think calmly for a moment. He doubted she would be upstairs with Henrietta and Charlotte, purely because of the difficulty that climbing the stairs would present her with. He decided to check on them anyway. Running up the stairs three at a time, he was soon outside the nursery rooms. William tapped on Henrietta's door and awaited her presence.

'Who is it?' she asked tersely, in a quiet voice. He presumed by the nature of her reply that Charlotte was fast asleep.

'It's Will,' he answered, and the door instantly flew open. Dressed in her long night-gown with her hair falling free over her shoulder she looked like his Hen of years gone by; not this matriarchal image she chose to hide behind to face a critical world.

'Did you sort them out?' she asked, her eyes betraying her anxiety.

'Yes, they will be going on a long journey and serving their countrymen well.' He smiled at her as her face relaxed. 'Are the two of you comfortable in your new rooms?'

He did not want to ask specifically if

Georgina was there because it would tell Hen that he had already been in her new bedchamber. She may not care, but he felt protective of Georgina. Her reputation lay in shreds because of his clumsy and selfish handling of the situation.

'Charlotte loves the room and she has gone fast asleep. I'm afraid I have another guest in the our quarters, but I did not think you would object to her staying with us.'

Although disappointed that his private time with Georgie had been lost he was relieved to know she was safe.

'Oh, that's fine as long as you are all comfy. Did you have much problem helping her negotiate all of the stairs?' he asked, wondering how she had managed. The leg was not that strong yet.

Henrietta looked surprised at him through her sleepy eyes, then smiled. 'No, not Georgie . . . Millie is here. She fell asleep on the chair talking to Charlotte so I wrapped a blanket around her and will send her to her own bed when she awakes.'

'That's fine, Hen. I'll see you at breakfast. Good night and it's good to have you both here with me.'

She hugged him and he smiled at her. Their family was together and that was his oldest and most blessed prayer answered. She went back to her bed and William ran back down the stairs. Perhaps Agatha would know what had happened to her. He made all haste to the kitchens.

As he approached the archway, William heard softly spoken voices and saw the flicking light from the oil lamps. Sitting by the large hearth was Agatha, Georgina, and a very tired-looking man. From the body language between the three, he guessed that this was the father, Bill Kell.

'So, this is where you are hiding!' he said, and saw them all jump up, except for Georgie who grabbed for her crutches. Agatha wisely prevented her from standing up. 'Mr Kell, I presume

— and sober, I hope?'

'Yes, I am he,' the man put his hand up to stop any protests from either Georgina or Agatha, 'I deserve your loathing, sir. I have been a poor excuse for a father and a husband, but I have asked the Lord to give me the strength to change. He helped me and I came here to warn you of the very real danger to your life.

'I will leave your home now, sir, and give you my wholehearted thanks for your care of both me wife and me daughter.' He turned and bent to kiss his daughter and then Agatha.

William stared at the ceiling for a moment as the man walked past him into the dark corridor. He then looked at Georgie's face, filled with hope that he would stop the man.

'Mr Kell, it is late. Agatha will make you up a bed in the empty store room and you can stay there tonight until I decide what should happen in the morning. At this moment I am too tired to make any more plans and need to go to bed, as does your daughter, sir.'

William saw the two women looking apprehensively at each other.

'Tell me, ladies, what have you got hidden in the empty store room that has you so stricken at the mention of it?' He moved towards the hook where the store keys were kept.

'It's our Daniel,' Georgina said, and he stopped. 'Pa floored him. We left him in there to cool down.'

William looked at her. 'Your whole family has finally moved in under my roof,' he replied and made his way to the store rooms.

Agatha followed.

'We didn't plan it, sir. Things happen, and fate just comes in, and before yer know it . . . '

'Agatha, stop jabbering, please. I'll open the door and enter. If he tries to get past me you lock us in together. I am more than a match for that hot-head.'

'Take care, he has a mean punch,' Agatha told him.

'Believe me, I have a harder one.' William opened the door wide and peered inside staring in disbelief at what he saw.

William ran forward just as Daniel kicked the stool from under his feet. The rope around his neck was secured upon a hook in the ceiling used for hanging carcasses. William grabbed the youth's legs and held him up, taking the strain before the noose could tighten.

Agatha let out a shriek and grabbed the stool forcing her son's feet back on to it. William removed the noose and grabbed Daniel's shoulders making him stand firmly on the floor. He was near to tears and staring at Agatha who had almost broken down on the spot at the thought of what had nearly happened, no doubt. If William hadn't decided to check on him — it would have been far too late.

'Daniel . . . Daniel, whatever possessed you to try such a thing, lad?' Agatha hugged him. That was the action which broke him. He held his mother tightly and sobbed like a child. William folded his arms and watched the spectacle, moved and speechless. This family were full of constant surprises.

'I'm terrified of the coble,' Daniel sobbed, 'and the sea and the mountainous walls of water. Georgie is right. You should have let her continue to go out with Pa . . . not me. I can't help it. I have nightmares about the sea. I dream I'm being dragged under and can't get back to the boat. I wake up sweatin', shivering and scared.'

William stared at them in disbelief. Georgie had sailed on that treacherous sea. She was to him, truly amazing.

'O'Connor made me feel like a man — just for a while,' Daniel explained.

'He used you, you fool,' William said, as he untied the noose and collected up the rope.

'Yes, he used me. I was of some 'use' to someone just for a while. But once I had created the image of being a man in his eyes, I ceased to be one in the eyes of my own parents. I blurred my father's mind with drink but, Ma and Georgie are too quick witted to be fooled. Tell me, rich man, as you stand there in judgement of me — no doubt calling me a coward once more — what is the use of a fisherman who hates the sea, is terrified of the water, and who only wants to draw?'

He looked at his mother. 'Ma, I struck you out of despair and drink. If I could undo that I would, but I can't. I never want to do anythin' like that again. I'll marry Sally if she'll have me for I've used her poorly too. But how the hell will I feed her?' He looked at the rope in William's hands. 'I let everyone down, constantly. I hurt or disappoint them. I never wanted to do anything ever again.'

William threw it into the corner of the store room. 'That is not a coward's way out. It takes a great deal of strength to kick the stool away yourself, but it is selfish. Your ma . . . ' William shook his head amazed that he was starting to speak like them. 'Your mother would have come into this room in the morning and discovered your twisted cold body. Is that how you would have said sorry to her for the wrong you have done her?'

Daniel shook his head, still holding on tightly to Agatha. 'I didn't know where else to turn, there seemed no way out of the mess.' Tears rolled down the youth's face.

'You want to draw?' William asked.

'Yes, you may laugh . . . '

'I am not laughing! It is a very great gift if, in fact, you are able to do it well.' William looked at him firmly.

'Yes. I can't help myself. But it won't put food on the table, will it?'

William ushered them out and back to the kitchen. He disappeared whilst the family were emotionally reunited. When he returned he was carrying the lamp from his study and a pen, ink and paper. He placed them on the table.

'I will give you one chance and one chance only, Daniel Kell. If what you say is true, sketch me anything. I will make allowances if your hand is shaky this night, but do a quick sketch and prove what you say is true.' William stared at him.

All eyes rested on the bemused Daniel as he precariously picked up the pen. He felt the quality of the paper then sat down as if everything that had gone before had never happened and, with an excited glint in his eyes, he sketched from memory a coble, ropes, nets, an inn, cottages and Georgie walking along the beach.

It was a quick line drawing, accurate and even the motion of the waves rolling upon the beach was captured in this monochrome sketch.

William picked it up, studied it, then sat down and scratched his head. 'You have a rare gift.' He looked at Agatha and Bill. 'You two tried to make the lad become a fisherman?'

'Drawin's don't feed yer,' Bill replied. 'Folks talked. He was always different to the other boys.' Bill shifted uneasily, and Agatha put her hand in his.

'Georgina was the only one who valued what I was, but you took her away from us,' Daniel said, and looked accusingly at William.

'So you would take your revenge on me and what you perceive as my 'class' by joining forces with rabble like O'Connor. You are both a tragedy and a fool.' William took hold of Georgina's hand. 'I have tried to right a wrong that I did to your sister by injuring her in the accident, no more, no less. If tongues have wagged to ruin her reputation down it is through no fault of ours. You owe your sister an apology!'

Georgina, who had been sitting stock still as if watching the theatre of her whole life unfold before her eyes, looked at William and could neither smile nor cry. She squeezed his hand not knowing how this could all be true. Even her Daniel had returned to them.

Life had never been so sweet. Yet she was stunned by his words. Had he only being righting a wrong — mending a wound? What she had taken for affection . . . love, was borne of a guilty conscience. How could she believe otherwise as their stations in life were so far apart.

'I will discuss this with Georgina later when I ask her properly, but for now, I shall explain something to you all briefly and finally. Then no more will be said on the matter. I represent your class, not from the fishing folk but from the earth — the miners. I worked hard, lost my parents and learned to survive.

'God presented me with a benefactor, an education and the opportunities in life to make something of myself. I took them and am now reunited with my family as you are with yours.' He turned to Daniel. 'So do not judge me!'

Daniel looked down.

'You can work here. We need builders, and I appear to be three short. Then when you have repaid some of the shame you have heaped upon yourself, you and I will discuss your ambitions and what route you can take to learn your craft. Yes, you can make a living from art if you learn the craft well and know what to do with your work.

'I shall help if you prove to us all first that the Daniel we hear tonight before us is for real and not just another mood or whim. Time will tell, but this is your one and only chance.'

Without waiting for a reply he turned to face Georgina. 'You need to go to bed. Say goodnight to your family. I'm sure that the cook can find safe lodging for them. And Daniel, you ever try a stunt like that again and I promise you this — I will let you swing.'

Daniel nodded again.

It was with a huge sigh of relief and a great deal of effort that the two tired people, William and Georgina entered his private room. The room was filled with books, a large desk upon a richly-coloured carpet. Its pile was deep and felt soft even under Georgie's boots.

This was William's own space where he relaxed in the chair by the open fire.

It had a male dominance about it. In the wall behind his mahogany desk was a panel, a door that opened into another personal space. Again a small fire warmed it.

Here a bed draped in rich tapestry covers and plush cushions had pride of place against a panelled wall. The rich thick drapes at the window, deep red velvet, made sure that this room was dark at night. Again the warmth of the colour made the room feel rich and cosy.

His slippers were neatly placed at the side of the hearth. He helped Georgie over to the bed, removed the crutches and turned back the covers to reveal crisp fresh white sheets. She felt them before she sat down.

'Do you expect them to be cold or damp, Georgina?' he asked her, a puzzled look upon his face.

'I still can't take for granted the feel or the beauty of everything around me. It is, like you, of such quality.' Her voice was almost in a whisper because much as she loved and admired everything about her, including William, she realised it could all be gone too soon. How could she stay within the house once her leg mended?

'I am tired Georgie, but I have already explained that I am from a far less affluent background than you see me in here. It is not something I enjoy discussing as it beings back many a mixed memory, an emotion, but I am neither proud nor ashamed of it. It is just a plain fact.'

She sat down, feeling emotionally drained and extremely tired. It had been a momentous day, one she would never forget. Her family almost fell apart, and yet they were now reunited. Her brother nearly hanged himself, and this man, William Phillip Carter of humble birth, had saved his life and offered them all a future. So why she feel so sad?

He removed her boots carefully. Then whilst still on bended knee he stared up at her with tired eyes and stared at her for a moment as if trying to read her mind.

'Millie is asleep already. Your mother is with her newly reunited family, bedding them down. So who shall undress you, Georgina? I cannot ask Benson, now can I?' He half smiled. 'I am a doctor . . . '

Georgina remembered her mother's words. She could be right. If there was any chance of a future with this man she could not lower her dignity.

'If you would undo my dress, sir. I should be able to manage from there on by myself.' She could feel her cheeks blushing.

'Very well, I quite understand.' He did as she asked and then stepped back whilst she held the garment in place with her hands.

'Thank you,' she said nervously, trying to be strong, for temptation was a tantalising emotion and she was all too aware that she had plenty of emotions flowing through her whenever he touched her.

He backed away to the door. 'I shall see if your mother is free, Georgina. Sleep well and we shall talk again tomorrow.'

'Goodnight,' she said quietly, adding 'William,' once he left the room.

★   ★   ★

The following morning Georgina was very disappointed to be informed by Henrietta that William had decided to leave the Hall early in the morning. She was seated at the breakfast table with Charlotte and Georgina, both of whom looked disappointed at the news.

'William says here, that he needs to oversee the building work and, if necessary, if he finds it wanting, he will then travel on to find new labourers. In the meantime he hopes that I, Henrietta, will see to all of Georgina's and Charlotte's concerns and cares.' Henrietta put the note William had left her down on the breakfast table and looked at Georgina. 'He has taken that brother of yours with him. I do hope the man can be trusted!'

'Daniel is a changed man,' Georgina said defensively. 'He wants to put right all the things that he has done wrong, or hasn't done right. It was never him that was bad, he just got in with the wrong sort through circumstance.'

'And your father? Has he changed, too?' Henrietta asked in a very terse manner.

'Yes, especially my father. He has realised he has not looked after my mother as a man should. He, too, will never slip back into his old habits.' Georgina looked up from the plate of food in front of her; her appetite had left her. 'Both of them are reformed and I am very proud of them both. It takes a strong man to admit that he was wrong and I have two within my family.' She looked straight at Henrietta.

'You have a remarkably versatile family, child. I congratulate you.' Henrietta sipped her tea and winked at Charlotte who smiled and blushed at her mother's teasing.

Georgina was still sensitive to all that had been happening and was bitterly regretting turning William away from her, quite coldly, the previous night. She must have hurt him deeply if he could not face her this morning. No wonder Henrietta was a little short with her. Here she had her family united at last and Georgina had managed to separate them so soon.

Georgina knew then that her days at Carlton House were numbered. Too many women under one roof made for trouble when there was only one man. They all would expect a share of his attention. She vowed to herself that she would exercise her leg and make herself strong, then she and her mam could start a business in the town.

Ma could cook now. So surely they could do something together. She smiled at Henrietta trying to convince herself that she had been very fortunate indeed. She should be nothing but grateful to all of this family. It was their home and it was she who was the interloper, or incomer whom the villagers called strangers.

Georgina had a fleeting image of her and her family being caught in a void, between the Hall and the town's folk. She no longer belonged to either world. What was she now? She should be enjoying this unprecedented gesture of hospitality, her family united, so why did she feel as if her world was falling apart?

Five days went by before William finally returned. Georgina saw him ride along the drive from the library window. He looked magnificent as he galloped Titan almost up to the Hall's steps. She stayed where she was, so that Charlotte and Henrietta could greet him alone. They had chatted to her, embroidered, walked and discussed elements of what Henrietta thought a lady should do or be.

Georgina had learned a lot from just listening. Apparently, Charlotte was to marry the following spring, so the lessons were really for her, but Georgina listened quietly fascinated, but realising where her limitations lay.

She read on, or rather stared at the book in her hand aimlessly. How she longed to run to him and see his face again.

'So this is where you are hiding, G . . . Miss Kell,' he greeted her politely as he entered, looking around him as if to make sure they were alone in the room.

'Not hiding, sir, reading,' she answered, and smiled warmly at him.

'Do you feel strong today?' he asked.

'Yes, I have been out for walks . . . well, quite short ones.' She looked at him standing only a few feet from her. She stood up and walked over to him. 'Did you manage to find your men?'

'Yes, I did and what is more I have set your brother to work.' He smiled broadly at her.

'He's not a coward, or lazy, he just is like a puppy surrounded by wild foxes,

he's in the wrong place. His tempera-
ment and his gift is befitting someone
who can live a more gentle life,
admiring the beauty around him. He is
no more a builder than a fisherman.
Although I pray he does not have a fear
of heights as he does for the sea.'

Georgina could see there was humour
in his eyes. Was he mocking her?

'Dear Georgina, how you care for
that wastrel touches me deeply.' He put
a finger to her lips. 'No, do not defend
him yet again. I have given him a
chance. He is now in York, working
as an apprentice to a cartographer. He
shall be expected to work long and hard
for his keep and a small remuneration.

'I have arranged for him to attend a
class of a respected artist one afternoon
per week. If in two years time he has
dedicated himself to his tasks and
proved he is a reformed character then
I shall sponsor him to go to London to
make his mark. If he wastes his chance,
he can make his own way in this world
and shall never be welcome here again.'

He looked tenderly at her. 'So tell me, Georgina, am I being fair or hard?'

'You have given him more chances than he deserves. I hope he does not let you down, sir.' She turned to the window, ashamed at the thought that Daniel might.

'Your father will be working on the estate. He is helping with fish of a different sort. The ornamental pools are being stocked afresh. I think it will be a fine occupation for him to have — an interest more than real work. Henrietta has informed me that your mother is a far better organiser of the stores and kitchen than her predecessors.

'However, her culinary ability is limited, so we will be hiring in some expertise, so that your mother can focus more on purchasing and organising stores.' He walked over to the window seat and sat down leaning against the wall, looking up at Georgina. He looped a finger casually into her hand raising it up, so that he could hold it in his.

'You have done wonders for my family, sir. I can never thank you enough.' She looked down into his eyes. There was a playfulness there coupled with a sadness too.

'I do not want your gratitude, Georgina.' He kissed the back of her hand and she felt that same sensation well up in her body, that deep longing feeling. 'I think you already know what it is I want from you, don't you?' He stood up; his body so close to hers, he wrapped an arm around her waist and pulled her in to him. 'I want you, Georgina,' he said softly, as his lips found hers and they were lost together, in a momentary embrace.

'William, do you require a meal?' Henrietta's voice shattered the moment. Her question was spoken out as she entered the room. The two lovers separated instantly. William walked over to Henrietta and linked arms with her.

'Henrietta, I shall have something to eat, change and then I want to speak to you of our plans.' He looked back to

Georgina who had sunk to the window seat, staring blankly out of the window, trying to control her emotions and the hurt she felt deeply inside.

For now she knew the truth. He had arranged everything to make her family's life bearable, promising even, but the price of it all was her — he wanted her as his . . . ' Her eyes were watering and she could not help herself. How could she bear to have the man she loved use her, and never respect her enough to make her truly his? But for his family she would have no choice. What would her mother say or do if she found out?

'Georgina, I shall return within the hour. There is somewhere I wish to take you. Wear your warmest cloak.'

She raised a hand in acknowledgement as her words failed her. Once they had gone, the tears came silently. She had to find a way out of the situation, but sat still. There seemed no alternative but to swallow her pride.

Georgina collected her cloak and did

not wait the hour. She had to leave the Hall, just for an hour or so. Carefully, she made her way down the steps of the Hall and on to the drive. She wanted to cut through the oaks to the rise, from where she could look down upon the sea. Strange, she missed it as much as her brother hated it.

Georgina found her leg ached, but she took each step carefully and steadily. Occasionally, she leaned against the oak's rough bark as if regaining her energy from the solid ancient strength of the tree. She had lost track of time; it had been such a strong desire to escape that she struggled onwards, until she saw her beloved sea from the rise.

Bracing herself against the wind she held the cloak around her, breathing in the cold salt-laden air. Georgina could see her old home, the inn, and the boats banked on the flat sands, but she had no wish to return.

'Georgie! Georgie!' the voice echoed on the wind, at first not even touching her senses. Then as the sound of Titan's hooves striking the cold earth came nearer she turned to see a very anxious looking William riding straight for her. Memories flooded her mind as she swayed slightly.

The accident, when she ran out in front of this magnificent beast replayed in her mind to the point where they had collided and she had fallen and struck her head. She still remembered the sharp pain that had shot through her leg.

This time he stopped alongside her. Holding Titan's reins firmly in one hand he gently gathered Georgia to him and moved them back into the shelter of the trees, away from the piercing wind that blew inland from sea.

'Georgina, whatever possessed you to try walking such a way on your own too. Whatever is it that troubles you?' He wrapped the reins around a strong branch of the tree.

She looked up at him as he held her, feeling his warmth and presence and said simply, 'You did.'

'What!' He looked as though she had verbally struck him.

'I know you will not see it the same way as I. You have been more than gracious to my family and for that I am eternally grateful, but . . . '

'I told you it is not your gratitude that I want!'

He was hurt and she understood why he was angry with her, but she could not look at her man in the face again if she did not at least explain to him how his suggestion made her feel. 'I know what you want. You have made that quite plain . . . '

'You have not exactly shied away from my embraces. I presumed you felt the same way about me.' He defended his actions.

He was still holding her and she knew she could not deny it. 'Yes, I do. You know I do. If we were going to . . . I mean if our situations were different and it was possible for us to wed, then I would be the happiest woman in England, but I cannot just lay with you to repay a kindness, even if you did promise me a home and a future once you had found a proper wife. I just can't live like that.'

He released her and turned around, scratching his head with his hand. She had insulted him, by his reaction she could tell, as much as he had her with his offer.

William turned around to face her and Georgina was so surprised because he was grinning broadly at her.

'Dear, sweet Georgina. How I offend you with my clumsy way of dealing with personal matters. I apologise to you unreservedly. I had wondered if you cared for me out of a misguided sense of gratitude. I can see now that I couldn't have been more wrong. In fact, neither could you because, Miss Georgina, it was a proposal of marriage that I was going to make when Henrietta interrupted us.'

He bent one leg and on bended knee before her repeated his words, 'I want you, Georgina, as my wife. To be wedded to me and mistress of the Hall, nothing more, nothing less.' He held out a small box from a jeweller in York.

Georgina took it from him with a shaking hand and peeped inside at the amazing jewelled ring, and hugged him to her. 'But I'm from down there.' She pointed towards the town.

'And I'm from a mining town, so we shall both appreciate our home and how fortunate we are.'

William untied the reins and lifted Georgina up on to Titan's back. He stroked her leg carefully. 'Does it ache badly?'

'Only a little,' she said honestly, as he carefully climbed up behind her holding her securely. 'I love you, William.'

'Does that mean you accept my proposal?' he asked casually, as he walked the horse on through the trees and back towards the Hall.

'Yes, William.'

He kissed her neck. 'Then I declare, my love, we are both cured.'

We do hope that you have enjoyed reading this large print book.

Did you know that all of our titles are available for purchase?

We publish a wide range of high quality large print books including:
Romances, Mysteries, Classics
General Fiction
Non Fiction and Westerns

Special interest titles available in large print are:
The Little Oxford Dictionary
Music Book, Song Book
Hymn Book, Service Book

Also available from us courtesy of Oxford University Press:
Young Readers' Dictionary
(large print edition)
Young Readers' Thesaurus
(large print edition)

For further information or a free brochure, please contact us at:
Ulverscroft Large Print Books Ltd.,
The Green, Bradgate Road, Anstey,
Leicester, LE7 7FU, England.
Tel: (00 44) **0116 236 4325**
Fax: (00 44) **0116 234 0205**

Other titles in the
Linford Romance Library:

RETURN TO HEATHERCOTE MILL

Jean M. Long

Annis had vowed never to set foot in Heathercote Mill again. It held too many memories of her ex-fiancé, Andrew Freeman, who had died so tragically. But now her friend Sally was in trouble, and desperate for Annis' help with her wedding business. Reluctantly, Annis returned to Heathercote Mill and discovered many changes had occurred during her absence. She found herself confronted with an entirely new set of problems — not the least of them being Andrew's cousin, Ross Hadley . . .

THE COMFORT OF STRANGERS

Roberta Grieve

When Carrie Martin's family falls on hard times, she struggles to support her frail sister and inadequate father. While scavenging along the shoreline of the Thames for firewood, she stumbles over the unconscious body of a young man. As she nurses him back to health she falls in love with the stranger. But there is a mystery surrounding the identity of 'Mr Jones' and, as Carrie tries to find out who he really is, she finds herself in danger.

LOVE IN LUGANO

Anne Cullen

Suzannah Lloyd, sculptor and horticulturist, arrives at an exhibition in Lugano which is showing some of her orchid sculptures. There she meets Mr Di Stefano, who offers her a job managing the grounds of his estate and orchid collection. Working closely with Mr Di Stefano's right hand man, Dante Candurro, she falls in love with him — but overhears his plans to steal the Di Stefano art collection. Feeling betrayed by further deception, can she ever learn to trust him?